And then an enormous shadow, far larger than anything seen so far, became apparent just out of range of the lights. It seemed to surge and quiver with the movement of the probing columns. Morten realized suddenly what it was. The writhing probes were not a half dozen individual creatures. They were tentacles, extensions, of a single animal. This dimly seen shadow was the central body.

Morten strained his eyes to see it. He turned off the lights once to try to better distinguish the faint outline, but was left blinded in the darkness. He turned on the lights again and waited for the central body to move closer.

It was at least six meters in height, roughly globular in shape. The massive tentacles eased it forward slowly while they continued their incessant probing in all directions. At the edge of the clearing one of the tentacles wrapped itself around a twenty-centimeter tree trunk. The tentacles tightened and pulled.

With little apparent change in the creature's motion, the tentacle slowly bent the trunk of the tree until it uprooted and fell with a slow, graceful motion. The tentacle dragged it a meter or two and released it. The awesome power of those arms of gray, rubbery flesh chilled Morten.

"It's coming toward the ship," said Free. "What do you think it will do?"

LASER BOOKS now available wherever books are sold!

For more information see the back pages of this book.

RAYMOND F. JONES

THE KING OF EOLIM

COVER
ILLUSTRATION
BY
KELLY
FREAS

THE KING OF EOLIM

A LASER BOOK/first published 1975

Copyright © 1975 by Raymond F. Jones

ISBN 0-373-72012-2

Printed in U.S.A.

I

It was his parents' Friday night soirée. He never understood what that meant except it brought a lot of people to the apartment. Tonight the place was filled with them, all three levels. People always frightened him.

He could hear rivers of conversation bursting everywhere, loud, whispering—always insistent, penetrating, demanding. There was the sound of music as some of the guests played their own compositions. Tape players exposed other sounds, all of them meaningless to him and equally exhausting. He wished he could shut it all out and make it go away. He knew his father didn't like it much either, but put up with it because his mother demanded it.

He remembered he still had to tell his father about being made King today at school. King of Eolim. He looked towards the dresser, on which his crown lay. The little lights flashed on and off at the peaks of the gold plastic crown. He crossed the room and put the crown on his head again and looked at himself in the mirror.

He wanted his father to see it. What better time than now? All the guests would see it, too, and they would know he was King of Eolim.

His mother wouldn't like it. He had been sternly warned never to come out during one of these gatherings. But she never liked anything he did.

Freeman Bradwell was 16 years old. He hated to be described for what he was, "tall for his age." He was over six feet in height. He was lanky, but not skinny, and he had already developed the tall person's stoop, a kind of leaning forward that made him seem perpetually anxious. The glasses that sat on the high bridge of his nose added to the effect.

He hesitated a moment and thought about putting on his clothes, but then decided on just a robe over his pajamas. That would be all right. Everybody probably knew anyway that he ambled off to his room when the party started. They wouldn't think anything of his coming out in his robe. He glanced once more in the mirror and decided the robe added to the effect of the crown.

Little groups of people were congregated in the hall near his door. A large man was loudly explaining an obscure principle of art to a half dozen listeners grouped around him. His arms pumped up and down to enforce his words. Then he stopped suddenly, arms in mid-air, as Freeman Bradwell moved abreast of the group.

The boy saluted, the lights on his crown twinkling madly. He grinned. The big man who had been talking so explosively twisted his face into a weak grin in response.

"I'm Free," said the boy. "I'm King of Eolim. They crowned me King in school today."

The big man rubbed his hands together as if in placation. "I'm sure that's very nice," he said. "I mean, it's wonderful. Sure, it's just great!"

Free was conscious of the hush that swept behind him. They were surprised to see him, and that's the way he wanted it. He was tired of being sent away—even though it terrified him to be in the midst of so many people. His father had often told him the only way to get over that was to move out among them. Well, that's what he was doing tonight.

He approached the top of the stairs, hearing the whispers behind him. He heard a woman say to another, "It's *him*." And he wondered why she had to say it that way.

The knots and groups of people closed in on one another behind him as he made his way down the stairs. This was where the music rooms were, and he heard the sounds as people entertained one another.

He came to the piano room. Inside, a crowd of twenty-five or thirty people clustered about the instrument, at which a young man was playing something jolly and humorous. Free edged his way through the crowd until he stood by the keyboard. His lighted crown flickered defiantly. The laughter died away as the party goers became aware of his presence. The hands of the player stopped above the keyboard.

"Hello," the man said. He hadn't stopped smiling.

"I'm Free. I'm King of Eolim."

The pianist swallowed hard. His smile dimmed a moment, but he brought it back. "That's great, Free. That's just great." He turned to the keyboard, and his fingers picked out a tinkling melody that seemed timed to the flickering lights on the crown. "King of Eolim," he said musingly. "I didn't know there was still a land of Eolim." He began to hum.

"Freeman Bradwell
King of Eolim
King of Eolim
Long live the King
Long live Free!"

The others began to unfreeze now and sang along with rising enthusiasm and happiness. Free looked about. They were smiling. They liked him, he thought. They really liked him.

"Thanks," he said to the man at the keyboard. "Thanks very much."

"Thanks to you, King Free. A long and happy reign."

He left the piano room quickly, overwhelmed by their gesture. His father had been right. He didn't need to be afraid of all these people. They were willing to be his friends.

He passed other music rooms and came to the game rooms. The first was the big Universe room, which had been installed only a few weeks ago. Two men and two women were intent on this game. The goal was to build a universe of galaxies, solar systems, star clusters, and other objects within the space of the room. The universe was built of metallic spheres and particles suspended in a modified magnetic field within the ten-meter high room. Any instability introduced by new elements would cause the whole thing to collapse with a clatter on the floor. The player who caused the collapse was the loser, heavily ridiculed for his awkwardness.

The players worked intently with computers to determine where they could place a new cluster or galaxy without upsetting the equilibrium of the entire system. Free liked this game. He played it often with his father, and often he won. He didn't use the computers, of course. They were vast mysteries he would never understand. But he could usually tell where to place the items without all the intricate computations. By "feel" he said.

He stood in the doorway as one of the women players placed a star cluster deep in the center of a galaxy. She withdrew the tractors triumphantly and laughed in delight. "There! That puts our side a hundred points ahead."

Her companion nodded smugly at his opponents, who were already preparing their next moves.

"I'm Free," the boy announced suddenly. "I'm King of Eolim." He spoke to the man who was setting his tractors. "You shouldn't put that solar system there. It'll make everything come down."

The man turned, startled, and backed the tractors to a neutral position. "Who are—?" he began harshly. Then he stopped, his gaze softening. He was an older man, but his face was youthful and vigorous. "So you're Free. And King of Eolim. We're happy to know you, Free. You say my positioning of the solar system was off?"

Free nodded. "It should go a couple of degrees to the right of where you were going to put it."

"How do you know?" the man asked kindly. "I checked it on my computer, and that's what it tells me."

"I don't know," said Free. "I don't know how to use a computer. It just looked wrong to me. Maybe you ought to check it again."

"I'll do that." He sat down at the complex console of the mini-computer and began feeding in the data of his proposed addition once more. The data on all the rest of the elements of the game were already in the computer. He pressed the button to read out the answer on the screen. He frowned at the figures and turned to Free. "You're right. I made a mistake. But I don't see how in the world you knew that."

"It just seemed that way," said Free.

The man on the opposing team objected. "You can't make a change after you're committed to placement. You forfeit the game."

The first player smiled. "You surely wouldn't object if I took a hunch from the King of Eolim, would you? That ought to make for an unopposed position in any game."

"I guess you're right. He couldn't possibly have picked the right coordinates except by sheer chance, could he?"

The player adjusted his tractors and picked up the solar system once again. Carefully, he moved it to the coordinate position Free had indicated, and which his own computer had confirmed. He locked it in place with the magnetic field and removed the tractors. The adjacent systems shuddered a trifle as they adjusted to the new influence in their fields, but there was no catastrophic reaction.

The man smiled at Free. "We won that one, didn't we?"

Free nodded happily. He moved beneath the simulated universe under the domed, night-dark ceiling with its pin points of light that added realism to the scene of the players.

He stared upward, his gaze fixed on the metal marbles that simulated the worlds in the immensity of space. "My world is out there—somewhere," he said pointing and searching with his eyes.

The man bent closer to hear his almost inaudible words. "What do you mean?"

"I'm not from Earth," Free said. "Not many people know that. I haven't told many. I'm from out there. I can't see my world, but it's up there somewhere. I don't think you've put it in yet."

"What's the name of your world?"

"I don't know. I can't remember. But they called me the Star Prince. Some day I'm going back. Nobody knows that, either. But I am."

"Sure, Free. Sure you are. Your father will see that you get back to where you came from. Why don't you just let it stay a secret and not tell anybody else about it? They might think you're just making up a story."

"You don't think that, do you?" said Free in sudden alarm.

"No, of course not! I'm just saying there might be those who do."

"I guess you're right. I guess I shouldn't tell anybody else."

"Thanks for your help with the game move. I sure

11

would have lost that one, and now I think maybe you have helped us win the game."

"It's all right. I'm glad I kept you from making that wrong move. I play this game a lot with my father."

He left the room, the players watching him half sadly until he was out of sight. He moved to the stairs and hesitated before going down to the first level. His father and mother were down there. He could see his father now, standing in the center of a group that listened intently to Morten Bradwell's words. Now and then they offered comments or questions, but for the most part they were quiet as if listening to an oracle.

Free knew it was always like that. People listened to his father. They acted and shaped their lives on his opinions and assertions. It gave Free a warm feeling to watch his father, respected and honored. He would never be like his father, but he could be proud that he was the son of such a man.

Morton Bradwell was just past forty. His hair was faintly streaked with gray strands, but his face and body were as vigorous and unlined as when he was twenty. He was a Genetic Engineer, a Research Professor at the city's great college. Free had tried to understand what his father did, what his work meant, but he didn't grasp any more than Morton Bradwell's simplified explanation: "I just try to make people better and better—children better than their parents, and *their* children better still."

Free didn't understand how people could be any better than they were. People who came to the apartment on Friday nights were so beautiful and wonderful—the shining people, Free called them. That's the way they seemed to him, bright and shining. He supposed that two hundred of them, gathered together in the apartment, knew everything in the world. Two hundred of the shining people, picked from anywhere in the city, undoubtedly knew everything there was to know.

He hesitated still, standing on the top stair, one foot twisted around the post. Maybe he shouldn't have come. Even his father might not like his appearing in that group of big, important, shining people.

But then his father saw him. Morten Bradwell glanced up at the stairway, and a mere flicker of dismay, so slight that no one noticed it, crossed his face. He continued to smile. "Free," he called. "Come down, son. You don't need to stay up there."

The others turned, and Free saw *their* faces. But then they smiled too, just as all the others had. They would like him, too. It was just that they hadn't expected to see him.

He moved slowly down the stairs. He didn't see his mother yet. He hoped she wasn't near. Morten Bradwell strode towards the foot of the stairs as Free reached the bottom step. He put an arm around his son and faced the group. "I'd like you all to know Freeman, my son."

Free nodded, the lights of the crown twinkling. The group surrounding his father nodded greetings and continued smiling. No one seemed to notice his crown.

"I wanted to tell you," said Free to his father. "I got this crown in school today. They made me King of Eolim. It was great. They put me on a chair on a

13

platform and carried me all through the halls and sang songs and gave me this crown. I wanted to tell you before I went to bed."

"I'm glad you did, son," said Morten gently. "You were very thoughtful. I'll come up in a little while and you can tell me some more about it."

"All right." Then Free chuckled suddenly. "I was just up in the Universe Room. The man was about to blow the whole game. I showed him how to make his play. He didn't think I knew how to play."

"I'll bet you surprised him!"

"I sure did. He thanked me, too. The others weren't going to let him have the play, but he said it ought to be all right to accept the play of the King of Eolim. The other man agreed. I guess the King of Eolim has some influence around here!"

"Yes, he does," said Morten Bradwell. He swallowed hard, and his voice was quiet. "The King of Eolim will always swing a big influence around here."

"I'll see you later, Dad." Freeman turned away and moved back toward the stairs. The pointed crown continued blinking all the way up to the next floor.

Morten Bradwell turned again to his guests. They began backing away now. They saluted, nodded, made polite noises and took their farewells to other parts of the gathering. Only one companion remained beside Morten when the others had retreated. Dr. Bryner Cavner stood beside him, looking up the stairway after Free's retreat.

"That was quite a shock," said Dr. Cavner. "Most of them had never seen one before."

"My son—Freeman—?"

"*That's* your problem, Morten. You continue to

think of him as *my son*. If you had disposed of him you would have no such term to clutter your thinking and your feelings."

"I'm sorry, Bryner," said Morten wearily. "We've gone over this many time before, and I don't want to go over it again tonight. You understand, this has been something of a strain, even to me."

"I do understand. I don't see how you keep your equilibrium. But there's one thing I want to say that hasn't been said before. These people tonight have seen him for the first time. Before, he was only something that was talked about. Now they know. Face to face, they know what a Retard looks and acts like. People in your own field. People who can and will influence your own progress in your career.

"You are damaging yourself, Morten. I am confident that you can make no further progress in your field as long as you persist in this whim of keeping your Retard. It is just not consistent with the character of your position. I tell you this as a friend, Morten. And we have been friends for a long time. You know that, don't you?"

"Yes, of course I know it. I don't expect you—or any of them—to understand. But I'm not going to euthanize him. If he's a Retard, then so am I—he's part of me. We've gone over it a thousand times. I don't want to talk about it any more."

"I know. Neither do I. But remember, Morten, you're at the end of the road with this decision. You have nowhere to go from here."

. . . . nowhere to go from here.

Those words stayed with Morten long after Bryner had left, long after Free was in bed and the lights

15

were out and nightdarkness infiltrated the residence.

. . . . nowhere.

But he knew that that was not true. There was always an answer. And for the three of them, that answer would have the ingredients for changing the course of their lives.

II

They were alone in the main living room of the apartment. The automatic cleaning machines were restoring the rooms and disposing of the debris. Their faint whine was the only sound.

Morten Bradwell sat on one end of the sofa that faced the window overlooking the city far below. Arlee Bradwell, his wife, sat at the other end, as far away as possible.

"It was like an exodus," said Arlee Bradwell. "They couldn't get out of here fast enough. I looked around and suddenly everybody was gone. Most of them didn't even stop to say thanks and goodbye."

"They should have better manners," said Morten quietly. "It's not like engineered humans to behave so rudely. We'll have to take another look at the gene charts we're using. Of course, they're older models —virtually obsolete now. We'll have to take that into consideration."

"Be as sarcastic as you like. But those people are our friends. Influential friends who can determine the future course of your career and our status."

"Another fault of our genetic engineering, then," said Morten. "Such factors are supposed to have been eliminated long ago."

"But they haven't, so we're faced with the disgrace of having paraded our own personal Retard before all of the people who have the most influence in our lives. Why did he have to come out, anyway? I've warned him over and over to stay in his room when someone is here, and he agreed to it. And what was that silly crown he had on his head?"

"He was proud of it. He wanted to show it off. Particularly, he wanted to show it to me before he went to bed. They had declared him King of Eolim at school today. It was quite an honor."

"What does that mean? I never heard of it."

"You never attended the Common School when you were young. It's a barbaric custom that exists in some places—no one knows how it originated. When there is a particularly sluggish student in a group they single him out and force him to wear that crown, and they dub him King of Eolim, the lowest of the low, the stupidest of the stupid. They parade him around in a makeshift platform chair and ridicule him all day long."

"You said Free was proud of it."

"Yes. He didn't even know it was ridicule. He thought it was an honor they were bestowing on him because they liked him. He wants so much to be liked by his fellow students—and by everybody. He wanted the people here tonight to like him."

"And they could scarcely hide their revulsion."

"I suppose so. A Retard in our society is what

a leper once was, long ago." Morten Bradwell stood up and went to the window, where he stared out at the vast city that stretched to the horizon in all directions. "There were other things I had hoped to try. New possibilities open up each day."

"You've tried everything," Arlee said scornfully. "Drugs, radiation, electronic hypnosis, brain-wave alteration, training—forced and unenforced. Even surgical modification. If anything, he's worse for all your efforts."

"Yet—how can he play the Universe Game on a mere intuitive basis and usually beat a player who is skilled on the computer and knows the mathematics of celestial kinetics? How can he place a single element correctly?"

"I don't know, and I don't care! I just want to be rid of him. I don't want to spend my life known as the mother of a Retard." Her face was distorted by the intensity of her emotion.

"How can you hate him so much?" Morten asked in wonderment.

"I don't hate him. He's just a thing. I don't have any feelings for him. I hate the situation I'm forced into by his existence."

Morten watched his wife in wonder and dismay. He loved her. She was the perfect product of the science to which he had devoted his life. But there were some things about her which he didn't like.

These were things considered normal by the society his science had created. They were the mores by which they lived. The great idol they all worshipped was the Intellect. The perfection of thought processes. The capacity to absorb data and the readiness to

19

assemble new structures out of existing data. That was the one standard by which they all lived, and his science was dedicated to the achievement of that soaring goal.

For three hundred years Genetic Engineering had been an exact science applied to human beings. It was still an advancing science, for humanity was even yet far from the perfection that could be postulated, and this was why Morten Bradwell had made the decision early to devote his life to it. In the perfecting of human beings there was an ever expanding frontier.

The mapping of genes, their modification, selection, deletion, combining—was a world of ceaseless adventure with no limits in sight. The physically obvious things had been conquered easily, the deformations, disease, hereditary malfunctions. Aging had been slowed to a tenth of its customary pace for adults. A person of eighty was in his prime.

The assault on the intellect had come harder, but it had come. Intellects had once been on the threshhold of genius if they touched 140 on the old I.Q. scale. Freeman Bradwell was at that level—and he was a Retard, a specimen of the type that was normally disposed of by euthanasia before the age of 12 at the extreme.

The minimum socially acceptable intellects had to measure at least 200 on the old scale. The maximum soared to immeasurable heights.

Morten Bradwell thought of all these things as he looked at his wife. She had beauty. She had an intellect that ranged beyond measure. But she despised the son she had brought into the world because somewhere, somehow, a genetic accident had thrust him back to the intellectual level of his ancestors. Even physically he was not an appealing specimen, although there was no specific deformity. There was just no beauty in him by any current standard.

It was accepted—Arlee accepted—that such offspring should be consigned to euthanasia. The quicker the better. Perhaps there was something of a throwback in himself, Morten thought, although he had conducted research on his own genes early in his career to determine where any such defects might lie. He had found nothing, yet he did not share the same thoughts, the same beliefs as Arlee—as others who set the standards of his culture.

He had permitted his Retard to reach the age of 16 without euthanasia. "He's too old to be killed now," said Morten. "It would be considered murder at his age. The Centers wouldn't take him."

"A parent is permitted without censure."

"Would you do it?"

Arlee's mouth turned in bitter distaste. "That's *your* job!"

Morten Bradwell turned from the window and went back to his seat at the end of the sofa. He sat with his hands between his knees, his fingers laced. He watched them as if they were detached from his body.

"No," he said slowly. "Free's death is not my job. His life is my job." He looked up to his wife's face. "He's my son. The only son I'll ever have. Since he's a Retard the rest of our quota is cancelled. For me and for you there's only our son—Freeman."

"Even he doesn't consider himself our son!" Arlee exploded. "He prattles this nonsense about a Star

Prince. This ridiculous offspring of ours thinks he's a prince from some star out in space. That's the kind of mind your precious son has."

"Nevertheless, the truth is that he is our son—*my* son, if you wish to disclaim him. I gave him life, and I'll see that he continues to have life, even if it costs me my own."

"What are you talking about now?"

"This party tonight has shown me things I didn't realize before. Bryner told me I had reached the end of my road, that I had nowhere to go if I persisted in my decision. I hadn't fully realized it that way before, but he's right.

"The way everybody walked out tonight—they won't ostracize us completely, perhaps, but they are so embarrassed for us they can't confront the reality of our keeping a Retard. They'll shun us gradually, turn away. And it will show up in my work. I am at a dead end, just as Bryner said."

"So what are you going to do?"

"There's only one place Free could be accepted for what he is. That's out on one of the colonies."

"That's as meaningless as everything else you've said tonight," said Arlee crisply.

"No. The colonies don't hold to Earth standards. They differ greatly from one another, and from us. There are colonies where Free would be welcome."

"I don't see the advantage of sending him out there. He'll just die more slowly and more painfully than at one of the Centers—or than if you injected him while he slept. But as long as that would get rid of him I don't care."

"You don't understand," said Morten. "I didn't

22

say I would send him out there. I am saying I will take him there, myself. I will go with him—"

Arlee rolled her eyes to the ceiling in helpless exasperation. "I give up. A long, useless trip that might consume months—lost time from your projects —but if that's what you want, do it. Do it quickly and get it over with. I'll take a trip somewhere myself while you're gone."

"You still don't understand me. I'm not talking about taking him out somewhere and leaving him. I'm talking about going with him myself—permanently—making a new life out there somewhere for myself as well as Free. I'm going to give Free a chance at life even if it costs me all the rest of my own. He's my son, Arlee, and I love him. I don't suppose you will ever understand that."

Arlee looked at him in silence for a long time before she shook her head and said quietly, "No, I will never understand that. It's hard for me to believe you mean what you have said, but I know you well enough to know that you do believe it. The only question that remains is what of me—what of you and me?"

"I hope that you will come, too."

Arlee threw back her head and laughed. A kind of hysterical laugh, Morten realized.

"In a few minutes you hope I'll turn my whole life upside down and give up everything I've known. Just to accommodate that ridiculous offspring of ours."

"Yes," said Morten. "That's what I hope. Think about it. There's plenty of time."

"Oh, Morten—Morten—isn't there another way? Are you so determined to sacrifice your life that

23

there's no other solution for us? Why does Free have that much importance to you?"

"I've told you how I feel about him. But even if I had no love for the boy I would feel an obligation to help him achieve a life that has meaning. I hadn't realized before what I must do to achieve it, but this incident tonight has shown me very clearly. Will you come with us?"

"You will get sick of that kind of life. You won't be able to give up your work. You'll be back within months."

"We'll be known as the Retard Bradwells. Everyone will remember us as the family that was so retarded it chose life in the colonies instead of the life of research we already possessed."

"You're coming, then?"

"Damn you, Morten Bradwell, of course I'm coming! What else did you think I would do?"

III

Morten Bradwell gave as his official reason for the change a desire to pursue a study of the effect on a Retard of living in a matching culture. It made his sudden resignation palatable to a few, but the many who knew him best did not believe it. Ever since the night of the soirée Morten's friends had expected some catastrophic action. They knew anything Morten Bradwell did would not be mild. The announcement of his intention to emigrate to a colony, therefore, did not evoke much surprise.

Freeman Bradwell was overjoyed by the news. He could scarcely believe it. "It will be on my world, won't it, Dad? That man—the other night—he told me that you would find a way to take me back home. I didn't believe him. I thought he was just trying to say something nice to me. But it was true. How did he know? Had you told him we were going to move out there?"

Morten Bradwell looked at his strange son. "We'll try to find it—if it's out there, Free. But I'm not even

25

sure I know where it is. And if you don't—"

"Oh, but I'll know it when I see it! There's a forest of giant trees, and there's a grassy meadow, and a lake. And across the lake there are cliffs where they live."

"Who, Free? Who lives there?"

"My people. The people who made me their Prince. Dad—"

"Yes?"

"What will they think of me being gone so long from them? Maybe they won't want me to be their Prince any more."

"I'm sure they will," said Morten Bradwell reassuringly. "How long have you been gone? When was the last time you saw them?"

Free's brows puckered fretfully. "I don't know. It all gets so dark and fuzzy when I try to think back there. I just can't remember." He looked up, frightened, at his father. "Do you think there is something wrong with me? Is there something wrong with my mind that I can't remember?"

"No." Morten shook his head. "There's nothing wrong, Free. Everybody forgets things at times. It doesn't mean anything."

"I know!" said Free brightly. "Let's go up and play one last game of Universe. I know if I could see the galaxy and the solar system I would recognize them. I know just how they look—from out in space—"

It would be the last game. Tomorrow the apartment would be sold, and the game rooms and the music rooms and the libraries would all be gone. Most of their possessions would be given to their friends and colleagues. They would take only a few crates of their most valuable possessions. Mostly the thousands of books compressed onto tiny rolls of tape that would be virtually indestructible in any climate they settled in.

They came to the Universe Room. Morten adjusted the lights to reflect the starshine of outer space. Both he and Free liked best to play the game that way. As they placed galaxies and systems and groups in the depths of their own private space they felt a little like gods in their creation.

"You first," said Morten. "We'll build this last universe the way you see it. Maybe you will see and remember your own world out there somewhere."

"All right. I'm going to put my landmark galaxy way out here near the rim of space." Free manipulated the tractors and moved a tiny spinning galaxy out near the upper corner of the room.

He did it without concern for the computer that was idle at his station. Morten Bradwell bent over his keyboard and inserted the coordinates and the mass of Free's galaxy into the memory of the computer. He considered, as if in deep thought, and placed a group of galaxies up high near an opposite corner.

Free protested. "That makes the game go too fast, Dad, when you place a whole group at once!"

Unconsciously, Morten had to admit he wanted the game to go fast. Now that he had made up his mind, he wanted to get out. Get out as fast as he could and let no one see him leave. He wanted everything familiar over and done with. But Free he would live with for the rest of his life—

"I'm sorry, son. I'll take them one at a time after

27

this. Let's make our last game the best one we've ever had."

That pleased the boy. He grinned and put a tiny star cluster inside the group Morton had just placed. Morten would have sworn it couldn't be done. There was no possible way it could be done without upsetting the equilibrium of the group and bringing the whole thing down.

But it stayed. Free placed it there without benefit of computer or any other calculation, and it stayed within the group.

Morten stared at the miracle.

"Your turn, Dad," said Free with just a little smugness in his voice.

They played the whole afternoon, past mealtime, and into the night. When at last they had filled the entire limits of space they stood back and looked at their creation with admiration and a little awe. They had never created so fine a universe before. And the game was a draw. Neither had won—or both had won.

"Do you see it out there?" said Morten. "Do you see your world, Free?"

The boy shook his head. "I thought I did a couple of times, but it won't stay. I guess it's not really there."

Morten put his arms around the narrow shoulders. "We'll find your world, Free. If it's out there in the universe somewhere, we'll find it."

Ships to the colonies were infrequent. There was some tourist business, a little commercial activity, and some people who traveled both from the colonies and from Earth, each curious about the other. But the

28

colonies had independent status. Their colonial status had disappeared long ago.

The colonies had been long established. The youngest were at least three hundred years old. The oldest was almost a thousand. They had been set up when space transform techniques had made intergalactic travel possible. At that time Earth-type planets had been discovered on a wholesale scale, and the ever-present concerns about Earth's overpopulation had made colonization a centuries-long frenzy. The new ships almost drained the mother planet of its inhabitants, until it became necessary to enact laws forbidding emigration.

Enforcement of anti-emigration laws created turmoil of its own for two generations of Earthmen. The right to emigrate became a standard of freedom that was fought for bloodily.

By then, however, the new science of genetic engineering was beginning to show results, and the colonies were gradually forgotten in a new enthusiasm to make Earth itself a paradise of rational human beings. That had been three centuries ago, and now the initial goals of genetics had been reached, and the next quantum steps were envisioned.

Giving up his participation in these next-stage conquests was the price Morten Bradwell was determined to pay for his son Freeman.

There was mutual distrust and dislike that stopped short of hostility between the colonials and the native Earthmen. The colonials had no desire to emulate the mother world. The inhabitants of Earth were considered decadent and freakish, wholly inadequate to survive on worlds that still required a constant battle with natural forces. The colonials, in turn, were considered barbaric and far below Earth-men on the evolutionary scale.

They both determined, quite sensibly, to leave the other alone, maintaining only such minimal contact as seemed convenient to them both.

The ships that made the colonial circuit two or three times a year were, nevertheless, large. They made a wide swing through two or three hundred colonies, carrying goods for exchange and sale, and the hundreds of travelers, who embarked for their own purposes.

Morten Bradwell studied very carefully all that the libraries had available on the many colonies known to have been founded. He sat in his study for end-less hours pouring over the tapes transmitted to his scanner. The study itself fascinated him. He wondered with a kind of irrational nostalgia at the concluding words of many reports: "No further sign of this colony was found on subsequent visits."

He tried to imagine the fate of a small group planted in some distant galaxy, determined to make a new home to escape a crowded world. What had over-taken them that they should disappear so utterly? Disease which their bodies could not combat? Hostili-ties within the group? Visitors from other worlds? Chemical incompatibility that had not been dis-covered in the preliminary testing?

But all this had nothing to do with the goal at hand, which was to select the best colony in which to settle his family. The numerous volumes of reports were too massive to assimilate by visual scanning. He put a sleep-tab connection on the machine and digested the information at high speed during the nights while he slept.

Finally, he announced his choice. "It's a place called Randor," he said. "We have to reach it by a small courier which we'll rent on Illeban, the nearest place the big ship touches. Randor is small. It had only a couple of hundred thousand people at the last census, and it's fairly young. So it won't have gone too far from the familiar customs we know here. It should be almost like Earth—without some of our present disadvantages."

Arlee was uninterested. She knew the type of colony they chose would make no difference. They would be moving into barbarity and desolation no matter what the choice.

But Freeman was excited. He looked at the pictures Morten had taken from the tapes. Brilliantly colored photos of the distant world showed a pleasant place of ancient rural character. The people looked comfortable, contented, and happy. Their intellectual level, according to the report, was about equivalent to Free's.

The boy scanned picture after picture, laying each one down with reluctance and a sense of disappointment. Morten knew what he was looking for—a forest, a meadow, a lake. But they were not there. "It looks like a nice place," said Free. "I'm glad we're going."

It was not the one, but he didn't know how to find that special one, so there was no way of telling his father where it was.

"It's going to be a great place," said Morten enthusiastically. "We're going to enjoy it very much."

The ship was like a city. Free had never been to space before, and the idea of this vast structure, with its enormous population, soaring through space was somehow even more miraculous than the orbiting of an entire planet with its nations. A planet was bound. The ship was free to choose its course. Perhaps that made the difference.

The passengers were permitted to embark early, to become acquainted with their quarters and with the ship as a whole, if they chose. Morten Bradwell and his family took possession of their rooms two days before departure to give Free some familiarity with the ship before the bulk of the passengers came aboard.

The corridors and parkways were massive, almost like those of the great city-buildings in which Free had grown up. He had never experienced a real, open landscape outside the city-buildings, but he knew what it would be like. He was sure he knew. The parkways gave him a little understanding, and he had seen picture tapes of every type of landscape of the whole Earth as it was during the last ten thousand years. He knew what it was like.

One of the parkways aboard the ship even had a large pool of water, meant to resemble a lake. Free found it the afternoon of the second day. He sat alone on the bench beside it, watching the tiny fish in its depths and the pair of ducks that swam on it. No one else was in sight except one man who strolled slowly by and sat alongside Free. He wore a uniform, and it frightened Free at first sight.

But the man put out his hand and smiled gently. "I'm Captain Maynard, young man. We'll be spending the next several weeks together on this ship. How do you like our fish pond? It was installed just before the last trip."

"It makes me feel like I'm right back at home," said Free. He took the man's hand now, his initial fear gone.

Captain Maynard was a big man. His pleasant face was ruddy, and his thick hair was black. But Free had the impression the Captain was older than Morten Bradwell. His father would like the Captain, he thought.

"We need something like that out in space," said Captain Maynard. His eyes seemed to be focussed far beyond the confining walls of the great ship. "We need something to tell us of home."

Free hadn't expected to hear a man of space speaking so fervently of home. He wondered if it was safe to tell the Captain of his quest. "I'm looking for my home, too," he said at last. He gestured beyond the walls of the ship.

The Captain looked quizzical. "Oh? And where is that?"

"I don't know," said Free. "It was somewhere out there. They called me the Star Prince. And then I lost it. I don't know where it is anymore. My father is taking me out to the colonies to see if we can find it."

The Captain nodded slowly and firmly. "I see. You certainly have my best wishes. I hope you find it. But it's a big place out there. Big enough to lose solar systems in—galaxies, even."

"I know. I play Universe with my father. I know how big it is. Do you ever play Universe?"

Captain Maynard smiled broadly. "Not in your

way. I play it with this." He patted the seat on which they sat. Free understood he meant the ship.

"I guess that is a better way to play it," said Free. He thought of the awesome journeys the ship and its Captain had been on. "You've been doing what's real. All I've ever done is play a game."

"It's different," said the Captain. "That doesn't mean it's better. Would you like to see my world?"

"Your world—?"

"The ship. It's the only world I have." The Captain rose and extended a hand. "Come, let me show it to you."

For the rest of the afternoon Free walked at the Captain's side through the corridors and chambers and all the secret ways of the vast starship. He was shown the compact brain center, the control center, where the pilots and the flight engineers gathered data and made the decisions that guided the ship on its way. Banks of computers made soft, living sounds as the Captain and Free passed by. Engineers at their consoles inspected test trajectories offered by the machines showing how the ship might most efficiently reach its numerous ports of call.

"There are so many machines," said Free, "it doesn't seem like there would be anything for the men to do except start them."

"It's true we depend on the machines for many things. Computers pick our course, keep us on it, run the engines. But there always have to be men who know what the machines are doing—and who can take over if the machines break down. Completely unmanned ships have often been sent on tours of the galaxies, but that doesn't mean there were no crews. The crews were back on Earth, watching, measuring, making decisions. These machines are our tools. Men still run the ship."

Free looked in fascination at the console where the Chief Pilot would sit. From this point a man would tell the ship where to go and see that it was guided there by the computers.

Miles of cables and wires connected the control center with all parts of the ship. Free walked with the Captain through the massive ducts that carried these between every remote corner and the central control. They visited the life support sections, where air, water, and food supplies were stored in decentralized areas as protection against massive damage to one part of the ship but not the others. Here were the machines that recycled all the wastes of the ship and recovered usable oxygen and water.

Then the Captain took Free to the chambers that held the great, silent masses of the nuclear engines. Here were gathered all the atomic forces that drove the ship, and the converters that shifted its position in time and space as the velocity crossed over the barrier of the speed of light. Even in flight, the Captain said, the chamber was almost soundless. Only the whisper of a few pumps, and the click of switches gave any indication that the place was alive. But in those great domed structures within the chamber, the Captain explained, the sun-hot fury of atoms was turned into power that drove the ship at unimaginable speeds through space.

Free wished he could understand all these things. His throat felt choked as he looked out from his own private prison to a world he could not comprehend. Why could other people understand the worlds of light and gravity and atoms, and fashion such machines as these—and yet he was cast in a mold of stupidity that would scarcely let him reach out a hand to touch these things, much less comprehend their function and their fashioning.

Captain Maynard sensed his despair. He put a hand on the boy's shoulder. "There are many worlds, Free. For some people it's harder to find their own world than it is for others. I think you will find yours."

"Thanks, Captain. Maybe I can do it if enough of my friends think I can."

IV

Lift-off took place the following day. There were no direct vision portholes, of course, but the scene could be watched from screens located throughout the ship. Freeman Bradwell had the most privileged spot of any of the passengers. He watched from the screen in the Captain's bridge, next to the pilots' control center.

His father laughed when Free told him of the invitation to the bridge. "You certainly do get around in a hurry!"

"Captain Maynard showed me all around the ship yesterday. I'd like to see liftoff with him."

"Of course. Go ahead. I'm glad you've made friends with the Captain.

During the weeks that followed, Free spent many hours in the Captain's company. Morten Bradwell was grateful for the attention Captain Maynard was giving Free. He didn't understand it. He knew the Captain's ship duties were enormous. He invited the Captain to their suite to offer his thanks at a time when Free was not there.

The Captain sat down across from Morten and Arlee. "I had hoped to make it a point to get acquainted before now. My time is limited, however, as I'm sure you know. But I've enjoyed your son's company. I hope you don't mind my taking so much of his time."

"We're the ones to be grateful," said Morten. "He needs kindness. You know what he is, of course?"

Captain Maynard nodded. "I know." He was silent a long moment before he went on. "I had one myself, you see. My own son was a Retard."

"I'm sorry," said Morten.

"And what did you—?" said Arlee abruptly.

"What I was supposed to do. The same as everyone else. I allowed him to be destroyed because he was not up to the standards of the great and glorious human race that we have become."

"And you regret it?" said Arlee.

"With all my heart. I wanted to tell you how much I admire you and your courage in supporting one small human being against what our great human engineers have made of the rest of us."

"I'm one of them," said Morten. "I'm one of those human engineers."

"Forgive my bitterness," said the Captain. "You know there's nothing personal, but I think your science has left some wide gaps in its application to real human beings."

"I am inclined to agree with you," said Morten. "That's why we are here. My profession has made a world that cannot accept Free and his kind. I'm de-

38

termined to find him a world where he can have a place. But that's only one face of genetic engineering. There are others less repulsive."

"I'm sure of it." Captain Maynard rose to leave. "Perhaps you can tell me of them before the trip is over. I would like to be less bitter about my own experience."

Throughout the rest of the trip the Captain was a frequent visitor to the Bradwell suite. He related endless stories of experiences in space. He told about the worlds of the galaxies by which they passed. When the ship touched down to exchange passengers or cargo, he took the Bradwells on tours of the alien worlds. And always, he was kind to Free with a deliberate passion that opened to the boy a new world of friendship such as he had never known. Free seemed to bloom and grow under the kindly hand of Captain Maynard.

The approach to Illeban was felt with sadness by all of them. Morten Bradwell felt he had already reached his goal of finding a world that would accept Free. Captain Maynard's world would accept him. But that was not wholly accurate, either. It was Captain Maynard that had accepted him. Free needed a whole colony, a whole world of Captains Maynard.

"I wish I could take you on to Randor," said the Captain. "The port is much too small for us, however, and our trajectory and schedule would be badly thrown off by such a detour."

"It's not at all necessary," said Morten. "We'd planned to rent a small courier to get us to our destination. When we're settled we'll return the ship and hire a ferry back to Randor."

After the landing the Captain personally escorted them to the ship rental agency. He inspected the ships offered and rejected three before he pronounced one adequate for their trip. "These little out-of-the-way rentals often have nothing but junk that will barely get off their home world, much less make the trip. This one should be o.k." He put out a hand. "We won't be seeing each other again, but I want you to know what a pleasure it has been to know you during this trip."

Morten nodded. "We're grateful for all your kindness."

The Captain looked then at Free, as if seeing, grown-up, the child he once knew long ago. "Thanks to you, Free." Then, impulsively, he threw an arm about the boy's shoulder and clutched him close. "Find your world, Free!" he whispered huskily. "Find your world."

He turned and ran toward the car that would take him back across the field to the great spaceship.

The courier was frighteningly small after the mammoth space ship that had brought them from Earth. Their personal belongings almost overflowed the storage holds. Some had to be stowed in the lounge section and in the cabin deck.

In the nose of the ship was the pilots' compartment with stations for pilot and co-pilot. Since there was no co-pilot, Free elected to take that station for himself. It left his mother alone in the lounge of the cabin deck below, but Arlee didn't mind. She was utterly sick of the whole journey so far, and wished it had never happened.

There was a feeding station at the port. Food of a

quality and kind remotely resembling Earth meals was served. The Bradwells ate after loading all their belongings aboard the courier. Arlee picked at the food and left most of it. Free was excited by the newness and strangeness of it—the little spined fruit that crawled across the dish while waiting to be eaten. The fish or reptile that exuded white smoke, and the little things that looked like toadstools and tasted like cheese.

They returned to the courier and rechecked carefully the fuel, food stores, and baggage cargo. Everything seemed in order. They took their places and sealed the hatches.

Free was proud of his father as Morten took the pilot's controls. These were far less complex than the intricate array of controls in Captain Maynard's big ship, but his father took on some of the qualities of Captain Maynard as he sat before the instruments of the little spacecraft.

Morten checked with the alien controller of the spaceport in the universal code of spacemen. In a moment, he was given clearance for lift-off. He pressed the control lever.

Free felt himself being sucked into the padding of the couch. It seemed as if hands clutched him and stuffed him into the substance. There had been nothing like this aboard the big, gravity-controlled ship. Then abruptly it was over as his father cut the acceleration. He felt nearly normal again. Only about twice as heavy as he should be.

"That was a little rough, wasn't it?" said Morten. "There's no way out of it. These little ships just don't have all the fancy gadgetry the big ones do. We just have to take a run and a big jump to make it off-world."

"It must have been fun," said Free, "back in the days when spaceflight was just beginning."

"I suppose it was. Everything is fun when it's new."

Once free of the sun system to which Illeban belonged, Morten set the controls to automatic and he and Free moved down to the lounge on the cabin deck with Arlee.

Randor was located in a nearby solar system, but they had to pass through an intervening system to get there. It was a ten-day voyage.

They passed the time by reviewing the material about Randor, which they had brought with them. Free went over it eagerly again and again as if some magic lay in the place, waiting to reveal itself to him the moment he landed. Morten longed for the magic to happen. Free seemed to be coming alive for the first time in his life, and Morten began to have real hope the boy could have a life of normalcy for his level.

For himself and Arlee he was not greatly concerned. They could find an acceptable existence whatever the conditions of Randor might be. It would be harder for Arlee than for himself, but she had the capacity to adapt.

They entered the outer bounds of the intervening solar system on the third day of the flight, and Morten had to reset the controls to avoid a trajectory too close to the sun. From their position, Randor was almost in line with this sun.

Morten showed Free how he operated the computer to set the new trajectory into the guidance system after taking observations on this sun and on Randor's sun.

"It's just like the game of Universe, isn't it, Dad?" exclaimed Free. "You have to know just where you can put our ship without disturbing the planets and suns that are already there."

Morten laughed. "In a way, but it's really the other way around. We have to find a way through them without being drawn into paths we don't want to take. There now." He pointed to the line drawn on the chart by the navigational computer. "This is the way we will go. Here is the sun we're coming up to. There is Randor's sun, and there is Randor itself. We'll be there in six and a half days."

Free scanned the chart with his eyes just as he had scanned the space of the three-dimensional Universe game. "We come pretty close to something right here." He pointed to a mark on the chart beyond the sun nearest them. "What is that? Do we land there?"

Morten shook his head. "It's just one of the planets of this sun. We come quite close to it, but we won't stop there."

Free continued to stare at the chart. "If this were a game of Universe," he said slowly, "I would put my ship there."

A day later they had passed the sun and were moving toward the farther reaches of this system. During the sleeping period following passage of the sun they were awakened by an alarm. Morten raced to the companionway leading to the flight deck. Free followed close behind.

Morten Bradwell stopped as he caught sight of the

flashing light on the control panel. Then he moved slowly and deliberately to press a series of control buttons and switches. Finally, he pressed one more to turn off the alarm and the flashing light.

"What is it, Dad?" said Free. "Is everything all right now?"

Morten shook his head. "One of the four engine compartments has broken down. Its converter has opened up, and the compartment is flooded with hot fuel. I have opened it up and jettisoned the whole compartment into space, but it doesn't leave us enough margin to fly safely as far as Randor. I know now what Captain Maynard meant when he said these little out-of-the-way rentals have nothing but junk."

"What will we do?" But before Morten could answer, Free's face lighted. "That planet we saw on the chart yesterday—we must be nearly there. And we're going to have to land as quickly as we can, aren't we?"

Morten strode to the chart table and switched on the light. A tiny red spot showed their current position. Just ahead lay the planet that almost touched their trajectory. "You're right, Free. That's our only chance. I hope it's habitable." He began punching a series of buttons at the edge of the chart table, and then he strode to the communication panel and flipped a switch.

"What's that?" asked Free.

"I just put the coordinates of this planet on a tape and set up a distress signal that will be transmitted automatically. We can only hope that a Patrol ship may be somewhere in this sector and hear our call."

"What if they don't?"

"We'll be here a long, long while."

Arlee was standing by the door of the companion-way. She watched Morten as he diagnosed their difficulty and sent out the emergency call. As he slumped against the navigation table and turned to her, she said, "We're lost, aren't we?"

"Not exactly lost. From a chart standpoint we know exactly where we are, but no one else does."

"It's the same thing. Have we got a chance of making it to this nearby planet?"

"There's no reason we can't."

"But we don't know what we'll find when we get there."

"No, I'm afraid not. It's a complete unknown."

"It's going to be all right!" said Free suddenly. "It's going to be a good world. I know it is!"

"You don't know anything about it," said his mother bitterly. Her expression was one of accusation that if it weren't for him they wouldn't be in this predicament.

He sensed her accusation.

"How do you know?" said Morten kindly.

Free looked down at his hands and compressed his lips. "I just know it's a good place. The same way I know how to play Universe all by myself, when everybody else has to use a computer and all that stuff to tell them how to play."

Morten moved closer and laid his hand on Free's shoulder. "You play a good game of Universe. We'll see how this move comes out. Now, I'd like you both to go down to the passenger lounge and take couches there. Use the safety straps."

"I want to watch you land the ship," said Free.

"I need to be alone. This is something tougher than I've ever had to do before. Besides, your mother needs you at this time."

Arlee said nothing, but turned away to the companionway. Free followed her, knowing she never needed him—anywhere, at any time. He wished so much that she did.

Morten Bradwell strapped himself in the pilot's couch and rested his arms on the control panels on either side. Six small screens were at eye level in front of him, flanked by scores of meters and instruments. The complexity of it—only a hundredth of that of Captain Maynard's ship—wearied him.

He pressed a button that gave him a view on one of the screens of the cabin lounge, where Arlee and Free were secure in their couches. They weren't talking. Arlee was staring unseeingly into the corner of the room. Free was lost in whatever fantasy he used to protect himself from the unresponsive world about him. Sometimes Morten wondered if he had been right in his decisions about Free. He thought of Captain Maynard. The space Captain had gone one way, and regretted it the rest of his life. Morten Bradwell had gone the other way—and wondered if his regret, in the end, might not be just as great.

He turned his attention back to the instruments. There were more urgent concerns than his personal problems right now. He watched the temperature readings of the remaining three converters. The reading of No. 2 had been above normal for several minutes. He had been aware of it with a sense of utter helplessness, knowing that if it continued he would lose No. 2 converter.

He glanced at the screen that showed the galaxy of stars beyond the ship. How had man ever gotten this far? he wondered. For a time man could control his own machines, but always there came a point where the machine took control—if by no other means than obstinately breaking down. He set the computer to calculate the flight pattern to the unknown planet if No. 2 did break down.

Arlee reclined in her couch and stared upward at the opposite corner of the lounge. She had not traveled in space very much, but she had done enough so that her senses told her the faint vibrations coming through the deep padding of the couch reflected serious trouble. She sensed that another engine unit was about to fail, and if that happened they were not likely to even reach the emergency landing they were planning.

She knew the strain her husband was undergoing as he watched the instruments of the failing ship. He was not an expert pilot or engineer. He possessed the average skills of his time, which would enable him to pilot a working ship and make landfall on routine journeys. And he had all the intuition he had helped breed into the race, but still he lacked the long experience needed to guide his instincts in such emergency. Arlee wished he had asked her to take the co-pilot's position that she might be near him at this time. It's where she wanted to be. It's where she ought to be.

It was where she would have been if it weren't for Free. But then, if it weren't for him they wouldn't be in this situation at all. She glanced at the boy and wondered momentarily what he thought and felt, but she could never hold such a consideration very long. She couldn't believe he felt anything. He had never been real to her. She had never been able to think of him as a living, thinking, feeling human being. She often wondered how Morten could do so when he understood, far more than she, what went into the makeup of a Retard, She thought of Captain Maynard and wondered at his eternal regrets about his own Retard son.

The reactions of the Captain and of Morten were not normal. Society had long ago determined there was no value in the Retards. Yet she sometimes wondered about her own feelings. Was it normal for her to be so completely without affection for her own child, even if he was a Retard? But if there were something wrong with her, then it was wrong with the whole society. That simply could not be.

Free watched the stars through the port. The room was dim enough that their light penetrated in ghostly majesty. They were stars unfamiliar to Earthmen, but Free felt he knew them. Somehow, out here the bands of ignorance and stupidity fell away and he felt he knew and understood.

It was an illusion, he told himself regretfully. He could not comprehend any more than he ever could the principles by which this ship was constructed and by which it flew. But these great principles were lesser things, he thought. He knew the more important ones.

But he looked across at his mother, her eyes staring at the corner of the room, and knew it wasn't true. He didn't know the things that would make her understand and like him. He felt her distaste for him like an imprisoning wall. Everything he attempted to do was made black by her despising. He didn't understand it. He didn't know what he had done. Once he had asked her, "Why do you hate me so much, Mama? What did I ever do to make you hate me so much?" And her face had just grown bitter as she turned away without answering him.

He wondered what the new world would be like. He could almost see it when he closed his eyes. But not quite. He saw his mother was worried about it, fearful that it would be a place they could not endure. He turned to her. "It's going to be a good world, you'll see. We'll like it there. Maybe even better than Randor."

Her eyes looked at him a moment. The same bitterness and despising. Then she looked away again and stared at the corner of the room.

No. 2 converter flamed with a devastating fire that sent the indicator off scale. Morten Bradwell had been watching, hoping vainly that it would not happen, and knowing it would. He pressed the jettison control before the indicator had completed its insane surge. The fuel, the converter, and all its associated machinery were propelled into space. The empty converter chamber remained open to space to cool the inflamation that had threatened the ship.

With only two units remaining, Morten knew their chance of safe landfall was slim. The remaining engines would be strained to capacity to brake them into the planet's gravity even if the engines were in top shape, which he knew they were not. All they could do was try.

"Arlee—Free?" On the screen he saw them turn.

"I just had to dump another converter. We've got two left. It's going to be touch and go."

"You'll make it," said Free confidently. "The other two engines will be all right."

Morten smiled. "Just like playing Universe, huh?"

"Just like playing Universe," said Free.

Morten told himself there was no logic to it, yet the boy's unsupported confidence infected him with a feeling that they would succeed in making safe landfall.

"We're entering the final trajectory toward the planet," said Morten. "We'll know in a few hours."

Free grinned. "We know now, Dad."

The crippled courier inched slowly into the new trajectory that turned it directly toward the unknown planet. The ship was poorly equipped with analytical instruments, but there were temperature sensors and water and oxygen detectors available. Morten turned the low-power telescopic screen toward the planet and aimed the sensors in the same direction.

The planet was still too far away to show much visual definition on the screen, but the sensors gave tentative readings that were highly satisfactory. Atmospheric oxygen was twenty three percent, just a trifle over that of Earth. Water was present in the atmosphere, the overall humidity was about forty percent. Heat appeared to be that of an average summer day on Earth. Gravity was 0.9 Earth.

It was too good to be true, Morten thought. It would be difficult to find more Earthlike conditions. Of course, there could still be scores of factors that had not been measured and which could inhibit any form of life. There could be large amounts of noxious gases in addition to the oxygen. Weather could be devastating. There could be unknown strains of bacteria and viruses, which no Earthly medicine could combat.

Their chances were still a good deal less than even.

For the next few hours Morten used the engines as little as possible, letting the ship fall under the gradually accelerating gravitational influence of the planet. Only when it became necessary to slow the ship's fall did he apply power again. And when he did so he felt a sick emptiness in his stomach. No. 3 converter was showing abnormal temperature rise.

He computed the rate of fall that would allow minimum use of the engines and set these figures into the control circuits. This was all that could be done. There was nothing else but waiting—waiting to see if they would reach landfall—or if No. 3 converter would fail first. He unfastened his restraints and went down the companionway to the cabin lounge. Arlee and Free were startled to see him.

"What's happened?" Arlee asked.

"We're not there, are we?" said Free.

"Everything is all right. The ship is on automatic pilot. I just wanted to see how things are with the rest of the crew."

"Just get us down on a livable planet and we'll be all right," said Arlee.

"We are going to get down all right, just like I told you, aren't we, Dad?" said Free.

"The ship is working fine. We've got a good chance of making it," said Morten. There was no use telling them now about the critical No. 3 converter.

He remained in the lounge a short time, but he did

not want to be away from the instruments long. He had to know the status of No. 3. Returning to the control room, he saw the temperature rise was continuing at a slow rate. He computed the point it would reach by landfall at its present rate. The answer was marginal. They might scarcely reach the surface of the planet by the time the converter disrupted.

After another hour and a half, the ship penetrated the outer fringe of atmosphere. Morten checked the altitude and took the first samples of atmosphere for analysis. The analyzer reported a nitrogen-oxygen mixture, much like that on Earth. Trace gases were inert. There was no sign of anything poisonous to human life.

He turned his attention back to the temperature indicators. Both of the remaining converters showed a sharp increase in temperature rise that coincided with entry into the atmosphere. And then Morten remembered. When the two converters had been jettisoned part of the heat shielding had gone with them. Now, those open portions of the ship's structure were exposed to the fiery impact of atmospheric entrance, and the remaining converters were being heated beyond tolerable levels.

A ship in such condition should be lowered at minimal rate. But that would require overloading the remaining engines. He lay back and watched the indicators climb. It was only minutes to the surface now. The radar altimeter showed seventy thousand feet, then fifty. The ship continued decelerating as it reached thirty, then twenty thousand.

Morten could see the landscape below. It was wooded, with open stretches. One of these looked like

52

a large lake. It was not directly below, but it was near.

Then, at ten thousand feet, the No. 3 converter temperature raged out of control. Morten jettisoned the engine chamber. The blast sent it careening over the distant lake, and it plunged into the water with a steaming explosion.

Simultaneously, Morten turned up the power of the remaining engine to maximum. The temperature of the remaining converter surged into the danger zone.

Five thousand feet. They were coming down too fast. Much too fast. He cried out to Arlee and Free, "Crash landing! Ready for crash landing—!"

The ship plunged and struck the surface. It bounced wildly and careened against giant trees, which flamed at its touch. Then it steadied, miraculously upright on its shattered base. It canted at an angle of almost fifteen degrees.

But it was down.

"I told you we'd make it!" said Free. He released his restraints and ran to the companionway and up to the control compartment. "I told you we'd make it!"

"You sure did," said Morten. He began laughing and threw his arms around Free. "You sure did. Now we've got to find out what we've made."

Then they heard the voice of Arlee on the intercom. "Morten—I need you. I think I'm hurt."

V

Morten and Free hurried down the companion-way to the lounge. Arlee had unfastened the restraints but she continued to lie on the couch, her face twisted in pain as she attempted to rise.

"It's my back. I think it was wrenched in the landing. Are both of you all right?"

"We're o.k.," said Morten. "Let me get the first aid kit. A contact X-ray will show if there is any dislocation."

Painfully, she turned over, Morten and Free helping her. From the first aid kit Morten took a roll of packaged film and pressed it carefully along Arlee's back. Then he pulled the red cord that released the self illumination of the pack. The internally generated X-radiation penetrated the flesh and bones, reflecting according to the density of the tissue and providing an accurate X-ray pattern.

Morten picked up the film and pressed the tab on the side to release the developing vapors within.

After a moment he stripped away the cover and examined the film.

"We're fortunate there's no dislocation," he said. "It's a bad muscular strain, but a few days in bed and some tight bindings will take care of it."

"Oh—I can't, Morten! I've got to help you set up base and find out what our resources are here."

"The best way to do that is get that muscle back to normal. Free and I can take care of setting up base."

"You've got a beacon call turned on?"

"It was still on before the crash. I doubt it is working now. Probably nothing is working. That's our next concern. But let's get you into bed in the cabin. We'll be careful. Free—"

Morten turned about, looking for the boy. He had disappeared from the room. Morten called up the companionway. "Free—we need you!"

"Where in the world did he go?" Morten complained irritably. "He surely didn't go below—"

"Never mind. I'm all right here," said Arlee. "I can move you myself—we can do it carefully."

"No. That would be worse than staying here. Wait for Free. He's probably gone outside."

"*Outside*!" Morten glanced about incredulously.

"He wouldn't understand that you have to make a hundred tests to determine if it is all right to go out. He'd just *go*—"

Morten had already turned and was running toward the lower level companionway. He passed the storage and the engine room levels, only partially conscious of the bent and twisted structure of the ship.

He reached the outside port and found the hatch swung wide open. The humid atmosphere, filled with the heavy scent of growing things, poured into the ship.

Morten felt suddenly weak at the awesome stupidity that had sent Free out into that unknown landscape with no protection, no prior knowledge of the hazards that existed out there. He faltered on the threshhold of the port and called Free's name at the top of his voice. He waited long moments. There was no answer. He tried again and again.

He might possibly track the boy through the heavy underbrush, but the chance of success was so slim that to attempt it would be idiocy equal to Free's. He closed the hatch against the possible invasion of some antagonistic species. When and if he returned, Free would have to pound on the door for admittance.

"He might not come back," Arlee said. "We might never see him again."

Morten refused to challeneg her. He didn't want to hear her say that was what she hoped would happen. "Let's get you into the cabin bedroom," he said.

She made no protest this time, but closed her eyes against the pain and clung tightly to him as he lifted her. Gently he carried her across the slanted floor to the bed in the cabin. He laid her carefully on the bed and then went out to find some blocks to prop the bed approximately level.

He had just finished when he heard the dull metallic clanging that echoed throughout the ship. He ran down the companionway and thrust open the hatch. "Free!" he exclaimed.

The boy was there, muddy and damp. His arms

were loaded with a mass of green foliage of some native vine. Morten balanced between rage at the boy's leaving the ship and relief that he had returned.

"Drop that stuff!" he commanded. "You know better than to make contact with the native environment until we've done tests to assure its safety. I explained it all to you during the flight. You didn't even listen to me."

Pain crossed the boy's face, and his eyes moistened. "It's all right, Dad. It's for Mom. It will make her back well. I brought this for Mom."

"What are you talking about? How is that stuff going to make her well? I tell you, drop it and let's get you bathed and detergentized against whatever irritant that weed may be carrying."

Free still held the leaves and vines clutched to his trembling body as if he hadn't heard his father. "We smash and grind the leaves, Dad. We make a paste with a little oil of some kind, and then we put it on the place where she's hurt. By tomorrow she will be all right."

Morten's mind went back over all the silly, childish things Free had come up with during his growing years. Things like this that sprang full-blown from his mind as if injected there from some source beyond the comprehension of any of them. "Where did you get the idea that these leaves would help your mother? There is no possible way you could know such a thing, even if it were true."

The boys mouth trembled. He spoke in a sudden burst of anguished pleading. "I *remembered*, Dad. I remembered the *ocana* vine would do such things. Don't you understand? We've found my world. This

58

is the forest and the lake and the meadow. This is where I was Star Prince. Only then there were great cities, multitudes of people—"

"Free!" Morten could not help the rage that burst inside him now. "You were born on Earth. Your whole life has been lived there. You were never Star Pr——"

His anger burned away as Free's face paled in uncomprehending anguish. He spread his hands helplessly. "I'm sorry, Free. I didn't mean that. We're in such a desperate situation here, and we've got to function as rationally as we can. I know you did what you thought best to help Mother."

"You'll use the vine then?" Free's eagerness melted some of the icy shock Morten's denunciation had poured upon him.

"I can't without testing it. It might be poison—"

"No. No—I tell you they're all right. I know—" He shrank again, understanding that his father did not believe anything he was saying.

"I don't think your mother would want it," said Morten kindly. "But I'll tell you what I'll do. Leave the vines outside, bring a small sample with you and we'll run a test to see if there's any irritant or poison."

Free hesitated, then dropped the bundle of foliage. He held out a single strand of vine to his father. "You can test it. It will be all right. If you only believed me—"

"I believe you, son," Morten said lamely. "I believe you. It's only that I have to make sure."

"You've never believed me. You've only pretended to."

Morten knew nothing he could say would penetrate Free's hurt at this time. He doubted anything ever would. He unpacked the laboratory equipment he had brought along for such testing as this. Within an hour he had completed his examination and found nothing noxious in the vine Free had picked.

"It's not poison or irritating," he told Free.

"Then you'll give it to Mother?"

"Why don't you tell her about it and ask her if she'll use it?"

Free shrank physically from the idea. "She'd never take it from me. I meant for you to give it to her."

Morten knew he was right. They both knew what Arlee's reaction to such a proposal from Free would be. "I'll talk to her. You wait here."

Arlee was enraged by what she considered the ridiculousness of the proposal that she submit to a poultice of "some weeds Free's demented mind seized upon out in the jungle."

Morten waited for her to become quiet. Then he spoke. "All right. Now you've had your anger. I had mine when I met him at the hatch when he returned. He's had about all he can take."

"So have I!"

"No. You and I will recover. But every ridicule and accusation we pile on Free just buries itself and stays. I came out here to try to find a life for him. We may be stranded on this forsaken planet until we die. So we're here in our own little world—we and Free. Let's try to make it tolerable for him."

"By letting him put a mess of stinking weeds on me?"

"Yes."

Arlee groaned in a mixture of pain and disgust.

"All right. I give up. Our whole lives revolve from now on around that misbegotten child of ours."

Morten paused by the door. "He's a human being, Arlee."

Free had been grinding the foliage to a pulp in the food grinder in the ship's galley. He had it ready when Morten appeared. "She doesn't like the idea very much," said Morten, "but she'll try it."

"That's all that matters," Free said happily. "She will know by tomorrow morning that it works."

Arlee did not even turn her face to Free as she submitted to the application of the poultice to the strained and damaged muscles of her back. Morten taped a plastic cover over it.

"You'll be all right in the morning, Mom," said Free.

Arlee remained motionless and unanswering. Then, abruptly, she stiffened and raised her head. "It feels as if I'm on fire!"

"That means it's working," said Free. "It gets warm, but it won't hurt. You'll be all right by morning," he promised again.

Arlee groaned and buried her face helplessly in the pillow. Morten motioned to Free that they should leave.

In the companionway Free turned to Morten. "Thanks, Dad. You'll see. I know you think I have crazy, stupid ideas, but you'll see this one works."

Morten laid a hand on his shoulder. "I don't think you have crazy, stupid ideas, Free. You have thoughts that are sometimes different from other people's. But they're yours, and they're precious to you. Don't

61

ever give them up just because somebody else doesn't understand. And that includes me. O.K?"

"O.K., Dad, and thanks."

It was apparent their distress signal sent out before the crash landing had not been heard. There would have been some quick response if a Patrol ship had picked it up. Morten made a cursory examination of the emergency beacon and saw at once why there had been no response. The transmitter had not been working even before the crash. The indicator lights had not shown anything wrong—but that was because they were defective also.

Morten closed the cover and slid the unit back in its rack. It was criminal to put such equipment on the starways, yet this was the best that Captain Maynard had been able to find at the rental agency. There ought to be some legal protection and enforcement for minimum safety requirements. But Morten knew there were not. They were far beyond the range of any law that Earth government could enforce. The rental agency was owned by terrestrials, but they had no respect or fear of Home Government in these far reaches of space.

"What's the matter?" said Free. "Can't it be fixed?"

"It's not likely. It wasn't working before we landed, and our crashing landing damaged it further. I'll look at it some more later, but right now we've got to see how we stand for survival."

"I don't think we've got enough food for more than a couple of weeks."

"Synthetics for two months is standard, but nothing I've see so far on this ship is standard," said Morten. With Free, he checked the food storage in the hold.

Free was right. The supplies would last no more than a few days, at best.

Free hesitated, avoiding Morten's eyes. Then he looked up, a sense of defiance in his face. "I'll get some food," he said.

Morten glanced sharply at his son's face. He was about to acknowledge and offer to go with Free. Then he understood what Free was asking—to be trusted to go out and contribute to their needs as an equal.

"Sure," said Morten. "As soon as it gets light in the morning. I've been watching the sun. It seems to move about the same rate as our own. The night should be about the same length as ours."

"Now is the time," said Free. "Morning will be too late. This is the time when the animals come down to the water. They go back to the forest in the daytime."

Morten wanted to protest that it was too dangerous, but he knew that Free had to go. "What will you need?"

"A light. A gun. A knife. I won't shoot unless I have to. The meat is better if it's speared. I'll make a spear if I can find a shaft."

Morten watched as Free made ready. He wanted to protest, or to order him not to go out into the unknown night. But he knew that if he did, Free would never attempt it again. It was something Free had to do.

When the boy was gone, Morten closed the hatch, but left it undogged. He returned to the cabin to see how Arlee was doing.

She was irritable. "I'll like to get this sticky mess off. I can't sleep with it on."

"How does your back feel?"

"Much better. Without this stuff it would probably have been completely well by now."

"Or much worse. Maybe Free's poultice is working."

"Oh, never mind! I'll keep it through the night. What have you found out? Can you use the beacon? Where's Free?"

Morten told her about the beacon and the fact that it had never worked. He told her of Free's night forage for food.

She was silent when he finished. Then she raised her head and looked at him, her face softening. "We're going to have to stay here. Our chance of rescue is just about zero, isn't it?"

"I'm afraid so. Except by some sheerly accidental landing of another ship, our only hope is the beacon —and that is pretty slim."

"You *will* keep working on it, won't you? You can't just give it up, ever. We have to keep trying, even if we know it's hopeless."

Morten returned to the pilot's compartment and sat at the console. Using their still-functioning emergency power—although he knew it must be conserved —he turned on the screen that showed the exterior landscape. Its infra-red response enabled him to pick outlines of the heavy forest growth and the shore of the lake not too far distant from the ship. He heard the night sounds of the forest, the grunt and chitter of animals. And he imagined somewhere out there his Retard son, stalking an animal for food.

Against the background of those forest sounds he allowed himself to look ahead, to the years of the future. The chances were a thousand to one that they were marooned here for the rest of their lives, as Arlee had suspected. And what would those lives be like?

It would be an existance of sheer fighting for survival for a long time. Finding dependable sources of food in the forest, and perhaps in the waters of the lake, would be their main task. They had shelter in the derelict ship for the time being, but its emergency power would last no more than a few weeks. After that, they would have to depend on open fire for heat and fuel.

But more important, what would they, themselves, become as those years passed? What had his great science of genetic engineering provided to sustain human beings under circumstances like these?

He supposed that soon they would have to examine the question of whether it was of value to attempt to sustain themselves indefinitely. How long would survival be of worth? It would be of value only so long as they could find interest in their existence on this world. The question of mere survival, devoid of all other values, was of no importance. If life became a burden to be endured, there would certainly be no value in enduring it. He was sure he and Arlee would agree on these questions.

The question they would not agree on—he was sure—was Free. What kind of life would Free find here? Morten suspected he might find a great deal more here than his parents would. If so, should they leave him alone at some future time? Morten wasn't so sure. He knew it would make no difference to Arlee, whatever the outcome for Free might be. But a life alone might be far less durable to Free than a life shared with his parents. Would they, in the end, elect survival merely for Free's sake? Morten knew he might, but felt equally certain Arlee would not.

The complexity of the question was infinite. It didn't have to be faced right now—but a confrontation with it would not be very far away.

There remained, of course, the possibility they might encounter some form of intelligent life here. With animal forms so abundant, and the planet so adaptable to human type life, that remained a very open possibility. They would have to wait for an answer to that one.

Six hours passed, with Morten's increasing apprehension. Then he heard the banging on the hatch below. He ran down and opened it. Free stood there, hands bloodied, and grinning. Behind him was the carcass of a large, pig-like animal which Free had dragged on a travois made of tree branches.

"We've got steak and chops!" Free said gleefully.

Morten nodden, grinning back at him. "Now, all we need is a refrigerator."

VI

Early the following morning Morten and Free left the shelter of the ship and surveyed the surrounding landscape. A gentle slope led to the sandy beach of the lake only a quarter mile away. Low underbrush and a few trees were in the area near the ship. And then they observed with awe that the ship had landed so that the heavy trunk and upper branches of one large tree provided support in lieu of the crushed under structure. The tree was completely charred from the ground to its upper reaches.

Morten examined the base of the ship apprehensively. "Our first job is to get some support under there. That tree won't hold it forever."

"We could be drying the meat while we do that."

Morten agreed. He almost wondered at the frequency with which he found himself agreeing with Free.

They stripped the carcass of the animal Free had killed the night before and cut the meat into long strips, which they laid over a drying rack they improvised from branches. Morten had eaten meat only once before in his life, and Arlee never had. He didn't know whether their stomachs could accommodate it or not, but they would have to try. There was no other ready source of protein.

After the meat was laid out to dry, they attacked the problem of adding support to the ship. A hydraulic jack—miraculously in working order—was among the ship's tools, and with it they managed to raise the low side of the ship and insert a firm rock foundation below it. Besides relieving the burden on the shaky support of the tree, this leveling made it much easier to move about inside the ship.

As they completed this task, Arlee appeared in the hatchway.

Free spotted her first. "Mom—you're all right!"

Morten waved to her. "I knew you'd be o.k."

Arlee came slowly toward them, after jumping from the hatch to the ground. "I feel fine today. All I needed was a good long sleep—and getting that sticky goo washed off me."

Morten put an arm about Free's shoulder. "I think we owe something to Dr. Free, here. His prescription seems to have done the trick." He was convinced the poultice had been effective in healing her strained back muscles. Without it, he was sure she would not have been able to walk this soon.

Arlee was unwilling to admit the possibility the poultice had helped in any way. She ignored Morten's effort at joviality. "What are you doing? You should be trying to get a beacon signal out, shouldn't you?

"That's a big job that has to come after we've made sure of our survival. We've made sure the ship

68

won't topple, and we've got some meat started drying. We've got to try to find edible plant food. And we should consider clothing of animal skins when we wear out what we brought with us."

Arlee stood beside him now, her eyes searching the distant shore across the lake, and the dense foliage behind and on either side of them. She looked at the column of the ship and the burned area of growth around it.

"At least two pieces of good fortune were with us," she said. "We didn't drop into the lake, and those trees kept the ship from toppling. Maybe our luck will hold and the beacon won't be as difficult as you think. We ought to minimize all other efforts to allow you time for work on the beacon. Let me help you out here. Just tell me what to do."

They finished the day working on a two-hundred foot clearing about the ship. They completed only a small fraction by nightfall, but they built a rough fireplace for cooking and for light. They stocked a pile of dry wood and brush nearby.

The work was different, but it was not exhausting. All of them were in excellent physical condition. It was a serious social error to be otherwise on Earth. Here, it was a necessity.

They ate lightly and retired early. They began to see the pattern their lives would take in the years to come. Beside Morten, in the darkness of their cabin bedroom, Arlee trembled with the sobbing that came upon her as she looked down the corridor of years before them. Morten put an arm about her to comfort her.

"I won't tell you I know we'll soon be rescued," he

69

said. "We have no way of knowing. But we'll do everything possible. I've been thinking: There's a medium size laser torch on board. We might figure out a way to use it to emit a beam into space and send a pattern of pulses with it. We might reach a passing ship that could detect it."

"What little chance of that!"

"Very little," Morten agreed. "You said we must try everything."

Arlee wiped her eyes and turned on her back. "Yes. I'm sorry," she said. "I know it's as much a disaster to you as it is to me. I couldn't help feeling for a moment what it will be like to never see another human being besides ourselves for the rest of our lives. We'll have no purpose except the mere staying alive."

Morten stared open-eyed into the darkness. "Is there any more purpose in twenty billion people being alive than in just three?"

They slept finally and rose the next morning to repeat the kind of routine established the day before: widening the circle of the clearing about the ship. Free found some berries and gourds which Morten checked for toxicity and found edible.

They made a fire that night, and Morten and Arlee sat by it, armed against night animals, while Free went on a hunt by the lake again to increase their meat supply. Within an hour he brought back another of the pig-like animals, which they would prepare for drying in the morning.

As the crackling of the fire died, they arose from the log on which they sat and started for the ship A pair of tiny moons appeared on the horizon beyond the lake. They had not seen these before. Together, they walked toward the shore of the lake to get a better view away from the trees.

The water reflected the rippling image of the little moons, but Morten did not want to go far from the circle of the clearing. He stopped, and they watched the reflections and the moons in silence. Around them the night sounds of the forest rose and fell. They could hear the wash of the water faintly on the beach.

From somewhere, across the shining expanse of water it seemed, another sound entered faintly upon the air. A rising, falling, chanting sound. A rhythmic wailing. It died away as the breeze shifted direction.

"That was almost like the sound of human voices," said Morten.

Arlee felt a chill. "Maybe there are humanoids here, after all." She shuddered. "And if there are, they're sure to be hostile."

"Why?" asked Free. "Why should they be hostile?"

"It's the way it's always been," said Arlee.

Morten objected mildly. "Not quite. Not all the time. But we don't know yet for sure what the sound was."

It came again, rising with the breeze off the water, carrying the day's warmth and the faintness of the sound. Whatever it was, the sound was distinctly like that of human voices. And somewhere, on the opposite shore, there seemed to be a pin point of light, flickering like distant fire.

"That means there are people here!" exclaimed Free. "We won't be alone, after all!"

Free didn't know, Morten reflected. The boy didn't know that all human beings were not alike. He had

71

never seen or learned the concept of aborigines or primitive humans with warlike instincts. "They may not be our friends—if they are truly human beings," he tried to explain simply.

"Why?"

"They may be poorly developed. They may hate and fear strangers. They may not understand how to read or to write, and they may have only very simple tools and weapons because they don't know how to make better ones."

Free glanced across the water towards the source of the sound. "They would be like me," he said slowly. "A whole city of them, maybe—just like me."

Morten felt himself floundering. "No, no. I don't mean that. They're what human beings used to be— before we learned how to make ourselves into what we are now."

Free continued staring across the water. "I know," he said quietly.

The sound remained faint. It became almost inaudible. The pinpoints that were like firelight died away, too.

"Maybe it was nothing," said Morten. They turned away and went back to the ship.

In the night again, staring into the darkness above him, he wondered about the things they had seen and heard.

Arlee was awake, too, turning about in nervous anticipation. "It really was native human beings we heard, wasn't it?" she said.

"Natives at any rate. How human remains to be seen."

"Maybe they're the remnant of some lost colony of

72

Earth. Or a secondary colonization Earth never knew about."

"It's possible. More than one such lost colony has been discovered. And scores of others are noted as lost with no signs of survivors."

"We have to consider their possible hostility. We could never withstand if they beseiged us for a long time."

"We have the boron guns we brought for hunting," said Morten. "They have a fifty thousand charge capacity. There's plenty of fire-power, but we couldn't spend the rest of our lives defending ourselves."

"All primitives are hostile, aren't they?"

"I don't know enough about it to say what the odds are."

"You've got to forget about the clearing, Morten. You've got to work on the beacon. It's our only hope."

The beacon was hopeless, he was certain. It was more important to establish living space for themselves now. But the presence of natives changed their situation. They would have to assume a defensive position was necessary—until they learned otherwise.

He turned over in irritation at his own apprehensions. They didn't even know there were any natives!

Arlee was already asleep, comfortably exhausted by the manual labor she had done on the clearing. Morten finally slept also. They awakened to the alarm set to the solar time of the planet. It was so near that of Earth, the difference was inconsequential.

Morten dressed and glanced out the cabin door. "I wonder where Free is? He's usually up and making noises by now."

"He can take care of himself," said Arlee.

Morten went to the other parts of the ship. Then he descended to the lower deck. The outer hatch was closed—except for a crack of light showing around its edge. And it was undogged. Morten was sure he had fastened it tight the night before. He stepped out and looked about the clearing. Evidently Free had the ambition to be out working on the clearing this early.

But Free was not in sight. The tools were not moved. Nothing had been changed from the night before. Morten decided to return to the ship to make another search. Then he glanced across the still, silvery water of the lake and remembered the sounds and the pinpoints of fire in the night.

He knew then what had happened. Free had decided to investigate for himself the possibility of human-like natives on the planet.

Morten groaned and leaned against the hull of the ship. His first impulse was to grab a weapon and try to follow Free's trail to bring him back. But he suspected the boy had been gone since long before daybreak, and Morten had no skill in following a trail through the undergrowth. It would take many hours to penetrate the distance to the opposite shore, trying to follow a path Free might have taken. If he had gone along the shore, his footprints in the sand might be easy to follow, but at some point he would have entered the forest, where it would be hopeless to try to track him.

Morten returned inside and found Free had taken a weapon and some food supplies. He hadn't gone completely unprepared.

Morten told Arlee about Free's disappearance. She

74

was unexpectedly sympathetic. "I'm sorry, Morten. But he seems to know how to take care of himself out there. He may come back all right."

"That's the first time you've ever had any concern for Free."

She shook her head sadly. "It's not for him. It's for you. I can't stand to see you torn apart by your concern for him. Why else did you think I agreed to come with you?"

He took her in his arms and held her close. "I'm grateful for that. I only wish you had some feeling for Free, himself."

He moved to the porthole and faced the lake. The waters were still and shining. The forest was breathless. Arlee watched his anxious scanning of the land and water.

"You should go after him," she said. "He may need you."

He turned in surprise. "There's so little chance. Will you come with me—?"

Arlee shook her head. "Then you would have twice the concern. I would only be in your way. I'll be all right until you get back."

There was a chance he might not get back. They both recognized it, but neither spoke of it.

"It's what you know you should do, isn't it?" said Arlee.

"Yes. It's what I've got to do. If Free comes while I'm gone, don't let him come after me. I'll come back if I can't follow his trail. And thanks, darling."

He made a pack of supplies for a couple of days. He took one of the boron guns and a radio to keep in close touch with Arlee. He put on jungle boots and lightweight trousers and shirt he'd brought for just such environment.

"I'll be no later than tomorrow night," he promised. "Whether I find Free or not."

VII

The animal Free had killed the night before was still hanging from the tree branch where he had left it. Insects were buzzing around it as Morten passed on his way to the lakeshore. The meat would spoil before they could get it cut for drying.

He searched for Free's footprints leading away from the clearing. He criss-crossed the ground in an ever-widening arc, swinging down toward the shore. At last, as he came to the sandy beach, he found it. A trail of Free's prints lead along the curve of the beach toward the far distant side. He glanced back toward the thick, squat column of the ship and waved to Arlee. He touched the radio control. "I've found it," he said. "It leads straight along the beach."

She heard him on the pilot's channel and watched him on the screen at the pilot's station. "Good luck, darling."

Morten remembered the brief image of the lake on the screen as the ship had descended. He remembered it as large, and now he judged the cliffs on the opposite shore of this arm of the lake as eight or ten miles away. To his left, the water extended beyond the horizon.

The ship was soon hidden by trees behind him. Over the water, scarlet birds wheeled and dove, in search of fish or whatever living things the lake held. The sand beneath Morten's feet was white and soft. In the forest, the foliage was brilliant green with a spectrum of bright flowers scattered through it. Only the unfamiliar shapes of the plants and leaves distinguished the scene from one that might have been found in tropical latitudes of Earth.

Morten speculated again that any human-like inhabitants must be remnants of a forgotten colony from Earth. In the days of frantic colonization, a planet such as this would have been a prime site for settlement. But if the natives were descended from Earth settlers it was no guarantee they would be friendly.

He moved rapidly, following the clear outline of Free's tracks. In some places the surf had washed them away, but it was easy to pick them up again on the other side.

The heat became uncomfortable as the sun climbed higher in the sky. It came almost overhead at noontime, and Morten wondered if there were any precession of the planet's poles to give a seasonal effect.

He stopped finally to rest and eat lunch. He opened two pliable containers, one filled with liquid and one with solid. He ate and drank alternately from them.

He and Arlee had lived nearly all their lives on synthetic fods. He didn't know how their systems would react to the changeover to natural foods on a permanent basis. But travelers and colonists had done it. He supposed he and his family could. There was the psychological factor, too, of getting used to flavors again, for the synthetics were purposely left flavorless. Once there had been an attempt to satisfy all tastes with a variety of flavors. So much variation was required that it was given up.

He returned the containers to his pack, anxious to be on his way. But for just a moment he lay back on the sand and closed his eyes.

It was like a whisper passing over him, and then the alighting of scores of insects. He opened his eyes and looked at the sky and the trees overhead through a mesh that was like fine fishnet.

He clawed at it with all his strength and twisted and rolled. It folded over and bound him, and then he saw it was being tied in place by a half dozen brown figures. His thrashing was useless. He was already bound.

He swore at his own carelessness in not keeping watch. But regrets were useless. As they bound him and left him on his back on the sand, Morten observed his captors. They appeared human enough to be descended from lost colonists, but he doubted they were. There was a primitiveness about them that couldn't occur in even a dozen generations of isolation.

The men were brown—more from the sun than from native coloring, he thought. Their long, black hair showed some attempts at grooming. They wore it straight or in braids, and with various small ornaments clipped to it. Their faces were clean, either by shaving or by nature. They wore clothing of animal skins, and these were as varied as their hair decoration and grooming. They carried weapons of clubs and spears, and bows and arrows.

There was animated discussion going on between three or four of the natives who appeared to be leaders. Morten was sure it concerned his disposition. He could not tell what the different proposals were, but in a moment the natives approached with a pair of long poles. They stretched another net between the poles and then picked him up and tossed him on it. Four of the men picked up the poles and began moving inland through the forest.

Morten inspected the fine threads of the net that lay over his hands. He twisted and pulled. The material cut into his fingers, but it did not break. It seemed almost like fine wire, but had the feel of fiber rather than metal. But curiousity about its nature now was useless. He was certain it couldn't be broken by hand.

The canopy of branches and leaves almost hid the sky above. They passed through thick undergrowth, and thick trees lined the way. A heavy layer of leaves covered the forest floor.

There was little conversation among his captors. He listened for familiar phrases and syllables, but none of their sounds seemed to bear any resemblance to Earth languages he was familiar with, and that included ninety percent of them. Language had been one of his hobbies.

For more than an hour the jolting travel continued. Then Morten observed a change in the surroundings. They came gradually into a large, cleared area in which was centered a village of primitive dwellings.

Women and children kept at a distance, but they stared in fascination at the bound captive.

Structures in the village were a mixture of cultural styles, Morten thought. There were very primitive daub and wattle houses, and there were moderately sophisticated structures of adobe and stone.

It was to one of the latter type that the group approached. Morten heard the grating of a door opening on some kind of hinges. And then he was thrust into a chamber a dozen feet square, illuminated only by a pair of high windows at least ten feet from the floor. His captors stood back then, spears and arrows aimed at him while one of the men slowly unbound the net that encased him. Once it was free, they backed cautiously to the door and closed it heavily behind them, leaving him alone in the barren room. The last thing he saw was the cylinder of his gun as one of the natives carried it out. He heard the sound of a ponderous wooden bar swung into place on the other side.

A single glance told him all he needed to know about the room. The dirt floor. The stone walls. The high, inaccessible windows. The smell. There was a thin opening in one wall a few inches from the floor. He guessed that food—if any—would be slid through that small opening.

He sat down with his back against the wall and fingered the button radio on his shirt. He should call Arlee. But what should he tell her? He didn't want her concern, and he didn't want her to try any foolish rescue efforts.

He grimaced at his own fears and worries. He knew Arlee better than that. He knew his own science of genetics that had produced her characteristics. She could certainly be trusted to receive knowledge of his capture rationally.

But he was saved the decision of initiating contact. The small button buzzed faintly, its center glowing with a pinpoint of light.

"Hello—I'm here," he said.

"I thought you would tell me something before now," said Arlee. "Are you all right? Have you found any trace of Free?"

"I followed his footprints for about ten kilometers along the beach. They were still very clear. Then I encountered some of the natives we heard last night. They surprised me and trapped me with a net. I am in a village about three kilometers from the beach."

Arlee had given a sharp intake of breath, but that was her only sign of surprise and dismay. "Are you hurt?" she asked.

"No. They haven't harmed me. I don't know what they intend, but they haven't been hostile so far."

"What do you want me to do?"

"Nothing. Stay in the ship. They may move in that direction and try to investigate the ship. Don't let them see you. Free may have been captured also, but I've seen no sign of him. If he should return to the ship, let me know at once."

"All right. Can you get your gun back? Can you escape without it?"

"Right now there's no way out of this stone cell. I can only attempt a break when and if they move me."

"With one of the boron guns I could wipe out a small village."

"No. You could never reach the village. I'm sure they guard the approaches through the forest too well for that."

Morten sensed her despair in the silence that followed. "I'm sorry," he said. "There'll be a way out. Look—there's something you can be doing. Remember I told you about that laser torch aboard the ship? You can be working on the modifications that will turn it into a beacon. Do you want to do it?"

"Yes, I'll try. Tell me what to do."

It was a very long chance. But it would give her something to do. She obtained the laser from the tool crib and for the next half hour Morten gave instructions on how to make changes in it and attach it to the movable antenna on the nose of the ship so the laser beam could scan the sky in the hope of attracting attention from a passing ship equipped to detect the beam.

A very long chance. But useful now to keep Arlee occupied.

She sensed the remoteness of success. "It would be a billion to one chance that a ship would encounter the beam and detect it."

"Our survival is a billion to one chance," said Morten. "If the laser works we will have cut the odds in half. We've got to take every chance there is."

"Call me every hour," Arlee asked.

"All right. I will."

"I love you."

"Thanks, darling. There'll be a way out. You'll see."

He didn't feel the optimism of his words. The inactivity became enervating. The atmosphere was stifling as the afternoon heat increased. He wondered if he was going to be supplied any water. In only a few minutes, however a flat clay pan of water was pushed through the opening in the wall. He raised it to his mouth. It smelled horrible, and particles of unknown substance floated on its surface. He closed his eyes and wet his lips and then swallowed.

The squares of light in the windows high above his head dimmed and disappeared in darkness as night came on. He realized he was going to have no light in his cell. Not that it mattered.

In the darkness he performed a vigorous set of calisthenics. There had been no food yet. Only the pan of stagnant water. He wondered if they were going to feed him.

A couple of hours after dark he heard again the sound they had heard from a distance the night before. The sound that was responsible for Free being missing and for Morten's captivity.

From somewhere in the center of the village there was the light sound of drums. It was irritating at first until he realized the sequence of beats was so complex that the cycle was repeated only after five minutes or more. With the drums there came the wailing of human voices. It sounded as if the whole village must be gathered in the central square.

There were periodic pauses and in those intervals he could hear the same sound as if in echo from some far distant place. But it was not an echo; it was another village, he guessed, intoning the same sounds. And as he listened he heard another and another. The forest must be filled with them. The population must be considerable.

And Free could be in any one of those villages, imprisoned as Morten was here.

He talked to Arlee while the chanting went on. She could hear it in the background. "That's the cause of it," he said. "If we'd never heard those sounds we'd be together."

"Or if Free hadn't gone away. Or if we hadn't come at all," said Arlee.

"All right, you win. There's no point in trying to assign causes. Did you have any success with the laser?"

"Very little. I can't understand what you want me to do with this wire coming from the red terminal. Tell me again."

For the next ten minutes they discussed the work, and then said goodnight.

The wailing chorus died away after another hour or so, and the village was quiet except for the crying of babies and the occasional squabble of a pair of voices raised in anger. He slept fitfully, feeling the frequent sharp sting of insect bites.

The morning light seemed to burst abruptly in the dark cell. Morten struggled to his feet, more tired than than the night before. He went through the calisthenics routine to preserve muscle tone in spite of inactivity.

After a couple of hours a breakfast was finally passed through the slit. It was a pasty, ambiguous substance as repulsive as the water served the day before. He forced himself to consume some of it and almost retched in the process. He threw the remainder in the corner. He reasoned they might cut off his rations altogether if he returned some of it.

The day passed as the day before it. He found a

pebble and marked the wall to keep track of the days. If there were to be many like this he could easily lose track. He conversed with Arlee for long periods, hoping that Free might have returned to the ship by now. But Arlee had seen no sign of the boy.

He rehearsed in his mind a dozen schemes for escape, each one seemingly as futile as the last. As long as he remained in this cell without contact with his captors there was absolutely no chance.

The second day seemed endless before daylight finally dimmed and left him in darkness again. The night chanting in the villages came again, and he talked with Arlee while it went on. Time seemed to be repeating the same day over and over.

The insect bites received the night before were swollen and painful now, and there would be more of them during the coming night. He knew of no way to protect himself from them. He didn't know where the creatures came from; they were absent during daylight. For the first few hours of darkness he spent much of the time fanning and beating the insects away. He slept again at last for a short time before daybreak.

Breakfast was once more shoved through the slit. Except for this, he would have supposed his captors had forgotten him. He had to get their attention somehow if he was ever to get an opportunity to escape. There was none while he lay in this cell.

He looked at the repulsive dish of food and decided to leave it untouched. Perhaps that would cause the natives to investigate. It was no sacrifice to leave it. The mere thought of eating more of the stuff made his stomach twist.

He talked with Arlee for a while. She was making good progress now with the laser, but she was becoming increasingly apprehensive about his imprisonment.

Near noon, Morten finally heard a sound he had been waiting for. The breakfast plate had not been moved from the slit, but someone was sliding the massive bar from the outside of the door. Morten stood up, his back against the wall opposite the door. He had no weapons, no strategy for attack or defense if they should come in hostile. He waited for the door to wheel open.

His muscles tensed involuntarily. Then the door was wide enough to see the figures crowding it. For a moment he couldn't see well in the shadows. Then he shouted, "Free—Free—!"

He ran forward and grasped his son in a tight embrace. The natives crowded behind. From the corner of his eye he glimpsed their primitive faces. "They got you, too!" he exclaimed to Free. "I had hoped you had escaped them and might return to the ship. But they got you, too!"

VIII

Morten backed away to inspect his son for injuries he might have received. "You're all right?" he said.

"I'm fine, Dad. But you don't understand—"

The natives were not backing off, arrows drawn, spears poised, as they had been when they brought him into the cell. There were no weapons at all in their hands. And they were grinning like innocent children.

Morten gestured toward the natives and turned to Free in bewilderment. "What—?"

"We're friends," said Free. "All these are my friends. They told me there was another strange man who had been locked up in one of the villages, and I hunted and hunted until I found the one, because I knew it had to be you. I'm sorry, Dad, that I caused you all this trouble. But you wouldn't have let me go if I had asked, would you?"

"No. No, I wouldn't. But I still don't understand, Free. How could you make friends with these people?

You have no language to understand one another."
He looked about at the apparently happy native faces
once more. "Can we go? Will they let me leave here?"

"Yes! We can go right now. Is Mother at the ship?
I hope she is all right."

"She's waiting," said Morten. "I've been trying to
figure out a way to escape. Let's go before they
change their minds. Tell me what's happened, on
the way."

Morten felt momentarily like an old man as Free
took his arm and escorted him through the throng of
grinning natives and led him out to the grassy court
between the village huts. One of the natives detached
himself from the rest of the group and followed beside them.

"Dad, this is my special friend. His name is Werk.
This is my father, Werk."

The native acknowledged the introduction as if he
understood the boy's words. Morten nodded, knowing the man couldn't possibly understand.

Werk looked young, perhaps not much older than
Free, but his bronzed body was massive with hard,
muscular contours. His broad face held an expression
of warmth and acceptance and understanding. Morten
was bewildered.

"Tell me what happened, Free." Morten struggled
to regain command of the situation.

"I wanted to find out if there were other people
here, that's all," said Free. "I knew they wouldn't
be enemies, like you thought they might. They would
be good, and they would be kind. I knew they
wouldn't hurt me."

"How did you know that? You had no basis for believing it."

"I just knew, Dad. I just knew. Don't you know how it is when you just know something? Like playing Universe and you just know where to put a piece?"

Morten shook his head. He didn't possess knowledge by any such medium as *just knowing*. Nor did he believe that Free did. Least of all, Free. At home, playing Universe with the boy, it had been a diversion to watch the accuracy with which Free could play, and to listen to him say that he *just knew*. But there were no diversions here on this nameless planet. Everything was connected with life and death and survival.

"They might have killed you," said Morten.

"They didn't. They acted like they sort of expected me. Like they had been looking for me for a long time. That's the way it was, Dad."

"All right," said Morten wearily. "Just tell me how you met them."

They proceeded rapidly through the forest growth, deep in the shadows of the great trees again. Werk led them unerringly until they could see the blue mirror of the lake, and the white sands of the beach.

"I went down the beach all the way to the other side near the cliffs," said Free. "That's where the main center of the people is. All these other little places like the village you were in are scattered through the forest. They are single families belonging to the oldest man still alive. When he dies, they break up and each of his sons then becomes the head of a family village and all those under him."

"You learned a lot about them in a short time," said Morten.

"When I came to the beach by the cliffs they were all sort of waiting for me. Like they knew I was coming. That's what their chanting had been for—to call me."

"You know they couldn't possibly have known any such thing."

"No, I don't," said Free earnestly. "Somehow they did know. Just like I knew they wouldn't hurt me."

"Why did they lock me up?"

"They didn't know who you were or what to do with you. They weren't expecting you."

"They would have tried to kill me," said Morten. "I *just know* that."

"They didn't want to harm you. They just didn't know what to do with you. They wanted me to tell them."

"How could they tell you all these complicated things? How could you know what they were trying to say? You couldn't speak each other's language."

They were walking on the beach, along the white sands that were turning golden under the afternoon sun. "When I first saw them I told them who I was," said Free. "I told them we had come from the stars. I pointed up to the sky and said I had come from a star so far away they couldn't see it. They understood what I was saying. They smiled and gathered around but kept a distance from me.

"They didn't try to touch me or threaten me. It seemed like they just wanted to hear me talk, so I kept on talking even though I knew they couldn't understand my words. I told them all about us. I told them about Earth, and our trip and our accident, and I asked them if we could be their friends.

"While I was talking I had this feeling they were understanding everything I said. Then, when they began to say something back to me I felt I knew what they were saying, too. It wasn't like understanding their words. I didn't understand them. I still don't. But I know what they are telling me. I just know. And that's the way it is. It's all I can say about it, Dad."

Morten felt sick in his body from the awful food he had eaten, and weary in his mind. He heard what Free was saying, but it was so meaningless. Part of the boy's defective mind was his intense belief in things that never could be true, things that had no reality. All his life Morten had tried to be tolerant of these imaginings, but their burden was becoming too great to bear. Somewhere within him was a weakness that shouldn't be there, but he couldn't help it.

Sometimes he wondered if Arlee had been right about Free and that he was the one who was wrong.

He realized suddenly that he hadn't even told Arlee of his release. He turned on the button radio and talked to her as they walked. Free watched him curiously as he reported that he and Free were on their way back to the ship. After a moment's more exchange he cut off.

Free looked at him. "Didn't she want to talk to me?"

Morten glanced at him quickly. All his life the boy had been aware of Arlee's indifference. He must even have been aware for a long time that she regretted he had not been euthanized. But now in this moment when he had been lost and had been found he had hoped blindly that she might want a word with him.

"She said she'd be seeing us very quickly," Morten fumbled. "She said she'd have something hot for us to eat when we get there. I could sure use some food, too. That filth the natives served me—did you eat with them, too?"

"I'm sorry," said Free, his eyes on the sand under their feet. He didn't say what he was sorry for. Morten wondered how many unnamed things his sorrow covered.

"What about your friend, Werk?" said Morten. "Why is he coming with us? What does he intend to do?"

"They have a word—I don't know for sure what it means. It's something like between friend and brother. Anyway, Werk has decided he is this thing—friend or brother—for me. He's going to stay with me."

"We can't have him in the ship."

An ancient defiance burst from Free. "He's not an animal!"

"Free, I didn't say he was. But he doesn't live the same as we do, and we haven't got the time to teach him any other way. His diet alone is different enough to make it impossible. I'm sure he has plans of his own as to what he would do. But the best thing is for him to return to his own people. Can't you persuade him to do that? You could visit back and forth frequently if you care to."

"He can stay with me!"

Morten had never seen Free so defiant. It astonished him, and at the same time was a little frightening. The contact with the natives had made some profound impact on the boy that Morten had never observed before.

They marched the rest of the way mostly in silence. The sun was hot and blinding on the sands that curved finally in a direction that must be south. They saw the partially cleared place where the ship stood poised as if nothing but man's decision prevented it from leaping into space again.

"There's Mom!" said Free. He was never quick enough to suppress the instant of delight the sight of her brought him. It was shadowed immediately by the ever-present memory of her indifference, but it never wholly died.

"Race you!" said Morten. Free took up the challenge and they ran along the sands until they reached the clearing. Werk ran beside them, striding easily, enjoying their game without comprehending it. Morten sensed the native could outpace them by far if he chose, but he remained beside them loping easily and laughing.

Arlee grasped Morten in a tight embrace as he came up. She buried her face a moment against his shoulder. She had been frightened, he thought, very frightened by the prospect that she might be the lone survivor.

She glanced at Free. "Your father could have been killed by those savages."

Free hung his head at her accusation and turned away to join Werk, who was looking at the clearing they had begun. Morten explained to Arlee who Werk was. "I'm not sure what we're going to do with him," he said. "Free insists he stay. He's very determined about it."

"You don't have to do what *he* says."

"I have to keep him from going off with them again." And he felt that's exactly what would happen if he forbade Werk to stay at the camp.

He told Arlee about his experience and about the things Free had related to him. "Somehow," he said, "Free has a kind of rapport with them that I couldn't possibly have. Yet it's ridiculous to believe they understand each other's conversation as Free claims. What kind or how much communication there is between them I don't know."

"It's not hard to understand," said Arlee disdainfully. "They are Free's kind. He's about on the same intellectual level they are."

"I thought I could understand things like this. But I've seen so many the past few days that I don't understand that I feel I'm not certain of anything."

"Come and eat. It should be ready now. The food you described to me could affect anyone's thinking. Call Free."

Morten glanced toward the edge of the clearing, where Free and Werk were busily expanding the area. "Let him stay with his friend a while. We've got to decide what to do with him if Free insists on his staying."

Morten ate and bathed and rested on the couch for an hour, after which he felt much better. When he arose and went outside again Free and Werk had almost completed a hut similar to the ones Morten had seen in the native village. Free was exuberant over their accomplishment.

"You won't have to worry, Dad," he said. "Werk and I have built him a house. He couldn't live in our ship, anyway. He says he couldn't stand being closed all around by solid walls. He'll be happy here. He'll show us better ways to get meat and fruits out of the forest. I like Werk, he's my friend, Dad. Please like him, too."

The boy's eyes were pleading in a way Morten had never seen before. Free had always accepted what he had been given and had asked for so little. Now he was asking something for which he felt more concern that Morten had ever witnessed before. Was Arlee right? Was it because Free had found his own kind?

"If Werk is your friend, he is my friend, too. He may stay, of course."

"Thanks, Dad! Thanks, so much. Werk says I can stay in his house, too, if I want to. Would you let me stay with him some of the time, at least?"

It was inevitable, Morten told himself. "Yes, you may stay some of the time with him."

Free and the native boy worked furiously in completing the clearing. This gave Morten the freedom to work on the ship, putting it in order to be their permanent home. At first he had supposed it would not do, that they would have to eventually move out and construct some kind of quarters out of forest materials. But it appeared far more reasonable to rearrange the space in the ship itself and make it their permanent quarters. By rearranging the storage and propulsion areas it was possible to obtain considerably more living space.

He completed the work Arlee had begun in order to convert the laser torch to a beacon. He mounted it on the nose of the ship on the antenna base, where it could be set to scan the sky automatically. He set the communication channels to automatic reception so an alarm would be sounded if any one detected the laser beam and tried to communicate with them. But they could not transmit a voice communication.

Not without the beacon.

Morten turned to the beacon itself. It was a delicate, complex piece of apparatus comprising intricacies of which Morten had no knowledge. He brought to bear all the inborn capacity that generations of genetic engineering had given him, but the complexity of the beacon continued to defy him.

He spent round-the-clock days with it, stopping only long enough to eat and catch a few minutes of sleep. He finally recognized this approach would not accomplish the goal.

At intervals he saw Free, who was constantly in the company of Werk. The two of them spent all their waking hours together, mostly on numerous construction projects in the clearing. A fire box, where proper cooking could be done. A watch tower in the heights of the tallest tree, the purpose of which Morten could not guess. A shelter, bigger than the first one, which Free and Werk now occupied together. Traps and lines for hunting, trapping, and fishing.

While his failure with the beacon mounted, another thought began to occupy Morten's mind. It began slowly, a mere wisp of an idea, and grew until it occupied his consciousness during every waking moment. At last he spoke to Arlee about it, although he readily anticipated her reaction.

They were watching the boys from the obervation port in the pilot's compartment, where Morten had established his workship. "They're always together," Arlee said. "I'm sure I was right. Free has found his own level in that savage."

Morten laid down his tools slowly. "You're more right than you know. It's among these people that Free is going to spend the rest of his life—after we're dead."

"Or after we're rescued? Would you leave him here if we get a chance to escape?"

"I've been thinking about that, too," Morten said. "I think the initial purpose of our journey has been fulfilled in a way we never expected."

"You agree that Free has found his own level here?"

"He has found friends—*a* friend, at least. He has found acceptance. By whatever unknown process that may be at work, he has found a strong affinity among these natives. He has found himself."

Arlee's face lighted with relief. "Oh, Morten—we could go, then! And we could both be at peace regarding Free."

"Yes—if we could go."

"There must be a way to get a signal out—"

"There's one other thing, first," said Morten. "An obligation we have—"

Arlee's face dimmed. "What obligation?" Her

voice held dread, as if any obligation, no matter how small, would drown whatever tenuous hope she had of escape.

"Arlee—" Morten turned and faced her. "We are never going to leave this place, you and I. We must function on that premise. I have no understanding of how the beacon works. I could not fix it if I did. The materials, the tools, the techniques are not available. It is only if some accidental landing should occur here that we might ever be found. We are overdue now and will be presumed lost in space. They do not send out search parties for such lost ones. Space is too big for that."

Arlee absorbed his words as an accident victim would await the impact of a crash he saw coming and could not avert. She had known the truth of what he was saying since their landing.

"And this obligation?" she said dully, her voice flat and emotionless.

"Someday there will be a civilization on this planet. The remote descendents of these people—and of Free—will practice genetic engineering on their own, and they will reach out to the stars in their turn. Maybe they will surpass Earth in peopling the Universe and understanding its mysteries."

"What has that to do with us?" Arlee said wearily. She watched Free and Werk in the clearing below.

"We can shorten the time of their development by a thousand—by ten thousand years! We can give them the learning, the science we carry in our own minds and in our library. If we leave with them what we know they can leapfrog a thousand generations!"

"How do you propose to do that?"

"We'll teach them. We'll set up a school. Even Free can teach some of the things he knows."

Arlee's eyes remained on him, scanning his face as if for something she hoped to find but knew she could not. "You're insane," she said. She turned away and went below.

IX

Morten didn't know the purpose of life. He was aware there were those who debated the question, but no Class IV human he had known had even considered it a meaningful question. It was like asking the purpose of the stars.

Of course, the question he and Arlee were interested in was not really the same. The question of whether one or two human lives should continue was not at all the same as asking the purpose of life. But now he saw an answer at least to the minor question. He and Arlee would have purpose. Their lives would have purpose—if they undertook to educate the natives—and Free—as far as they could go. It would be as he had said. Hundreds of generations would be jumped.

How long would it take them to develop writing if they were left alone? How long would it take them to measure the girth of their world? How long would it take them to build a glass and investigate the stars?

All that time could be shortened to a few months, a few years.

That would be purpose and meaning enough for him and for Arlee. He felt a flood of energy within himself supporting his concept. It seemed worthwhile. It seemed purposeful. It would give Free the best possible world in which to survive.

He found the two boys that afternoon drying some fish they had caught in the lake. Werk had shown Free a deposit of salt at some distance from the camp, and they were busy salting and drying the fish.

"You'll have enough meat and fish stored for us to last the next five years," said Morten.

"Oh, I'm showing Werk how we've been doing this," said Free. "They've never done anything like it. They won't eat anything that's been killed more than a day."

"Some of the stuff they fed me had been dead a lot longer than that," said Morten. "Does Werk like to learn things from you?"

"Oh, yes—but he teaches me a lot more than I teach him. He knows how to build all these things—" Free swept a hand around the clearing to indicate their constructions.

"How would you like it if we taught Werk and all his friends and family some of the other things we know? Do they have any written language? Do they know how to measure?"

"Can they read—? No, I don't think so." Free spoke to Werk, using an awkward mixture of Werk's language and his own. He seemed to get the idea across, but the native boy looked puzzled.

"He doesn't know what I'm talking about," said Free. "They don't know how to read and write."

"Suppose we teach them?"

"That would be great!"

"Reading and writing—we would have to make up a written language for them. We'd make it out of our own writing and adapt it to their sounds. Then we could teach them numbers. Do they know numbers and counting?"

This time Werk grinned enthusiastically to Free's question. He held up the fingers of his hands. "They count up to the number of their fingers," said Free. "They say that's all the numbers there can be. There can't be any more than the number of fingers a man has."

"We could teach them the truth. We could teach them how to measure the number of meters across the lake and how far it is to their sun."

"Oh, yes, Dad—let's do it! I know my friends would like that. Let's start a school." He laughed with sudden uproarious enthusiasm. "And I'll be King of Eolim again!"

Morten began with Werk. And for this he had to bring the young native into the ship, after all. He set up a tape recorder and got Free to guide Werk in pronouncing words for all the objects and conditions and actions he could come up with. After about five hundred words he found himself encountering the same sound over and over again, which he translated as *echling.*

"It means 'nothing'," said Free. "Anything they don't know or understand they just dump it in this

105

one basket they call *echling*. I think he's used up all the words he knows."

Five hundred words, Morten pondered. Maybe he had actually gotten only half of them, but, even so, a vocabulary of only a thousand words was impossibly primitive. How could they function as a society with no greater vocabulary than that? They would have to learn hundreds of new concepts as they went along.

It took him nearly a month to analyze the voice patterns of Werk's words. And Morten realized other natives might show quite different patterns for the same words. He wanted to get it worked out clearly for one specimen at least. He could modify it later.

He correlated the voice patterns with those of his own language as nearly as he could, and adapted the alphabet to those patterns. From this he formed a written word for each of those Werk had spoken.

The sudden intensity with which he found himself absorbed in this effort surprised Morten himself. There was a kind of unreality about it that he didn't dare dwell on. When he thought of it, even momentarily, he was a little frightened by the insanity of it: lost on a nameless world an unthinkable distance from Earth, committed for the rest of his life to educate a primitive tribe to a level of civilization.

It was Purpose. He had to keep that constantly in mind. Without Purpose, his life—and Arlee's could not go on very long.

He spent endless hours trying to convince Arlee. She felt he had tricked her in his assurance that Free had a place among the natives and no longer needed his parents. They were free to go. They were held back only by this new obsession to educate the natives.

The obsession had taken all her hope away. She did not believe the beacon was impossible to repair. If Morten spent the effort on it which he was lavishing on his educational program he could make the beacon work. She was certain of it.

Nevertheless, she agreed to assist in the school. It was futile to resist. She needed something to keep her occupied, anyway.

Learning five hundred words did not take Morten very long. He practised with Free and then with Werk in putting the words into sentences. The native language, however, did not concern itself much with sentences. A single word to indicate a want, or a pair of words to indicate an action or an object were usually all that were needed. Morten learned these combinations quickly, much to the delight of Werk. Although he became proficient in the limited vocabulary, and Werk told him there were no more words, it seemed to him that something was missing. Werk and Free seemed to enjoy an ease of conversation in the native language that was far beyond him. He had to realize, also, that Free had gained a considerable ability to converse in the native tongue during those first two or three days among the people.

He asked Werk then to communicate to his people the intention to hold a school and to get about a dozen of his friends and relatives to be in the first class. Werk agreed enthusiastically.

The prospective pupils showed up the next day. There were eight men and six women in the group. They were filled with the same enthusiasm Werk displayed.

The first task was to erect an open air shelter to serve as a schoolroom. Morten hadn't been able to find out yet if there were any major distinctions in the seasons. But if cooler weather developed, it would be easy enough to enclose the classroom.

It took them two days to build the classroom. A primary need was that of writing materials. Morten learned from Werk that there was a large leaf in the forest, which dried to a leathery consistency and which the natives used to draw pictures and doodles on with a stick dipped in a berry juice. Although they drew pictures in this way, Werk assured him they did not draw pictures for sounds, as he put it.

For himself, Morten had a small blackboard taken from the chart desk of the ship, with a supply of chalk. The day after completion of the schoolroom Morten faced his assembled students, who sat on the rough benches before the rough desks, with their leaf and berry juice writing materials. They watched him expectantly.

He smiled as he faced them. "This is the beginning of civilization in this place," he said in his own language. Only Free understood him and nodded, smiling back.

They called themselves a name that Morten had transcribed as Grook. He pronounced the first part of the sound and wrote a G on the blackboard. The natives looked bewildered. He pointed to the letter and grunted the sound. He wrote it again and repeated the sound once more.

Some of them began to get the idea. He heard a few grunts, and sticks were dipped in berry juice to duplicate his G on the dried leaves. Werk was the first. He had already gotten the idea of written language from Free.

Morten pronounced the second sound and wrote an R on the board. The response was quicker this time. All but one of the pupils immediately copied the second letter. One fellow was still puzzling over the G.

By the time he reached the K they were all with him. In fact, they were eagerly awaiting his formation of the final letter. They wondered if there was more, but Morten stood back himself now in great satisfaction and pointed to the pupils. "Grook!" he said.

He pointed to the word on the board. "Grook!"

A kind of joyous pandemonium burst out in the class. The natives stood up holding high their leaves with the badly scrawled word. They pointed to the word and laughed to each other.

"Grook!"

"Grook!"

"Grook!"

Morten had not anticipated such instant and uproarious success.

Free remained sitting at his desk with Werk. Each of them had neatly printed the word and held it up so Morten could see. He nodded to the two boys. They smiled back at him. Civilization *had* begun in this place, he thought.

He didn't try to hold them too long. He suspected rightly that their span of attention was not much greater than that of a six-year old child. He let them go after an hour, and they went off, back to their villages, waving their marked leaves to each other.

"They like it," said Free. "They like school."

Morten regarded his son. "Do you like it, too?"

"Oh, yes. Someday let's make one of them a King of Eolim!"

What limited learning? Morten had pondered that question all his life. He had sought in genes under the electron microscope for the answer. He had tried to manipulate and select those that would make a human being capable of learning anything and everything at electronic speed. He had succeeded to a great degree. But he didn't know why he had succeeded. And he didn't know why he had failed where failures occurred. There was still some great key he didn't understand.

He didn't understand why Free could not comprehend beyond a very low threshhold. In the days to come perhaps even the Grooks would surpass Free in learning. He didn't want that, he thought. That would only put Free in the same kind of situation he had been in on Earth. For a moment Morten wondered if his intuition to educate the Grooks had been a right one.

He wasn't convinced, however, that the schools Free had attended were competent. They had all used the latest electronic, hypnotic, chemical and other persuasive devices and methods. He had used his own, too. And always, Free had ended up crying out, "I can't! I can't! I can't do it—!"

Perhaps there would be other ways. Other ways he could develop to teach the Grooks and which would help Free. The opportunity for research here was tremendous. But all these were questions to be answered in the future. For now, he felt satisfied and confident he could plant civilization here. Free would be a part of it. Free would grow with it. He would take a mate from among the Grooks. Some of the women were quite pretty. And his children would be among those to reach for the stars from this unknown world.

That night he told Arlee how he felt. "They liked it," he said. "The idea of learning appeals to them. You can always tell when someone wants to learn or when he merely tolerates instruction. I saw it in them today, Arlee. They want to know things. They're eager to learn new things."

"Like inscribing their poor little five hundred words on a piece of dried leaf? Do you think that will make them any more immortal when their sun takes its turn at becoming nova?"

"You promised you would help, Arlee. It would relieve your mind of concern about our situation and give you reason and purpose."

"I'll help. What would you like me to teach them? Art and history of Earth?"

He knew she was ridiculing him now, but he needed her help. And she needed the activity, too. "We have to teach them all the simple things," he said. "How to make water wheels and windmills, wagons and roads and bridges and farming. Engineering, more than science, at first. I don't know if we'll ever be able to make paper. Can we get along with that leaf material they're using? So many things, Arlee. I need your help very much."

"I told you I'd help. But I want to go back to Earth, too. If I do this, promise me you'll keep working on the beacon, and that we'll go if we ever get the chance."

"I promise," he said.

The Grooks learned rapidly, just as he had supposed they would. He concentrated on expanding their vocabulary with words of his own language. He taught them the nature of their world, that it was a sphere, rotating in space about a giant sun.

This caused great consternation, because they had never conceived the idea of a spherical world. Morten reminded them how they could see farther from a high place and used the observation tower built by Werk and Free to refresh their memories. Then he showed them on the blackboard how this was possible, because the planet was round. They were very disturbed, and Morten realized he was on dangerous ground. He taught it with a light emphasis and let them draw their own conclusions. When they finally caught a clear picture of the idea they ceased to flinch and conceded it had to be that way.

Communication was the tool that had to come first. After that, the flood of inventions, tools, and devices could come. Before that, they had to learn how to express their thoughts and how to convey them to one another.

The Grooks were attentive and excited in the vocabulary classes. It was as if there had been some kind of void that this information was filling, as if they had long recognized the need but did not know how to satisfy it. They were equally adept at learning to write on the stiff, brown leaves with the colored juices. It was a fabulous game. They wrote words that Morten placed on the board and showed them gleefully to each other.

Then, one day, one of the men named Abol, whose massive hands clutched the sticks and the leaves with desperate awkwardness, asked Morten, "Why do we do this?"

Morten had been waiting for this. He sent Abol to the far corner of the schoolroom. He asked Werk to come to the near corner. Then he directed Werk to write a message: 'Come home at once.' He directed Werk to give the message to one of the girls to deliver to Abol.

The Grook accepted the message and scowled at it.

"Read it aloud, please," said Morten.

Abol pronounced the words stiffly, one at a time.

"There," said Morten. "You might have been, say a hundred kilometers away, and Werk needed you to come as soon as you could. He couldn't call to you, but he could send you a written message to tell you what you wanted."

"Merta could have told me what Werk wanted."

"True. This was a very simple exercise to show how a written message can be used to send information over a great distance. It might have been something more lengthy and difficult, which couldn't have been remembered by the messenger. Then the writing would be needed. Can you see how useful this is?"

Abol shook his bear-like head. "No."

The rest of the Grooks were also frowning, as if some great puzzle had been presented to them, which they couldn't understand.

Then suddenly Abol burst out laughing. As if infected by him, so did the rest of the Grooks. They laughed uncontrollably and hysterically. Morten made an effort to quiet them, but it did no good. Something had struck them as hysterically funny. Something connected with the demonstration he had offered.

He saw he wasn't going to learn what it was that day. Or regain control of the class.

"That is the end for today," he said abruptly. "Tomorrow, with the sun in the same place, we will come to class again."

They went, dancing and galloping off toward their forest villages, still hilarious over an unknown something. Morten was puzzled, but he dismissed it from his mind.

Tomorrow he would find out.

Only Free and Werk remained undisturbed by the hilarity.

The next day, with the sun in the same place, Morten returned to the classroom. Free and Werk were there, but no one else. Morten glanced at the sun. "They're usually early."

He waited another fifteen minutes. The two boys talked in low voices with each other.

"They aren't coming," Free said finally.

"How do you know that?"

"Werk says so."

"How does *he* know?"

Werk looked up for a moment and then back at the floor. He shuffled his feet and finally stood up, moving toward the center of the room and then pacing slowly back again. "You wouldn't be able to understand, Mr. Bradwell," he said. "I don't know how to tell you so you understand. It's like when you taught us to write words on a leaf with juice. It seemed like something wonderful, and then you told us yesterday what it was for and it seemed so useless and like what you call a joke that nobody is coming back again, ever."

Morten felt an apprehension of something he couldn't name. He sat down on the rough chair by the table. "Why do you say it is a joke?"

"Because it is so—so clumsy—" Werk searched desperately for words. "Our messages do not need a dry leaf and a funny picture. When a man wants his son he thinks of his son. Then, wherever his son is, his son knows his father is thinking about him. And then they think about what they want to say to each other and that is all there is to it. They have no need of useless leaves with markings, and someone to carry them to a distant place."

Morten felt limp, as if the sun beating on the roof of the schoolroom had turned unbearably hot. "Telepathy," he said.

"I do not know that word."

"I don't either—not really," said Morten. "Can they do this, no matter how far apart they are?"

Werk nodded. "It doesn't make a difference."

Morten turned to Free. "Is this how you and Werk understood each other so quickly?"

"I don't know for sure. I think it is, Dad."

Morten turned back to Werk. "But the writing of words is much more than this. The words on the leaf can be read long after the man who wrote them doesn't care to speak—even when he is dead."

"We would not want the words of a dead man," said Werk firmly.

"I have so much more to give than this," said

Morten. "Get them to come back, Werk. I won't make them write words on leaves if they don't want to. I will show them other things."

The Grook shook his head again. "I could not get them to come back, no matter how much I tried."

"Then get another group and we will start all over again."

"They know about it all over the villages. They are laughing, and no one will come ever again."

"I can give them the fire and the lightning to be their slaves. I can give them the stars."

"You give us too much," said Werk. "You give us things we do not want. Things we do not need. Things we already have. We have the stars; they light our sky at night and we watch them and know they are great mysteries we can never find out. Can anyone have more than this?

"We have fire, and it is a terrible thing that is sacred and to be used no more than is needful. The lightning is a terror we do not want. So you see, Mr. Bradwell, there is nothing you can give us. We have all we need. I am so sorry. It has been a little fun, learning your words and the writing game.

"But it is enough."

X

Werk left with the promise he would return soon. He didn't explain why he was going, but it seemed to Morten that for the moment the boy could not endure the world of the Earthmen, which had been thrust so overwhelmingly upon him.

When they were alone Morten said to Free, "Do you think it is true, what Werk said? Do you think he speaks the mind of his people or only himself?"

"It's true, Dad," said Free solmenly. "When any of them speak on important matters it is the mind of the people, because, just as Werk said, they all know what everybody thinks." He came closer and stood before Morten. "But does it matter, Dad? Maybe Werk and his people are right—for them, at least. Does it matter so much if they never write books or have cars on long, straight roads through the forest or have telescopes that can tell the distance to the stars? Maybe what Werk says is very true: they have all they will ever need."

The boy looked down and smoothed a patch of

the rough dirt floor with his toe. "Maybe it's simply that they are like me," he said.

Morten felt torrents of confusion in his mind. He had pinned such great hope on the ability of education to civilize and humanize these primitives. But a gift could not be given unless it was received. "We've got to find a way out of here," he said decisively. "Your mother was right. We've got to find our way back to civilization."

"Dad—" Free looked at him hesitantly.

"Yes?"

"I like it here. I like Werk. I like the Grooks. They like me. I know they'd let me stay. If you and Mom go—would you let me stay here?"

Morten felt an impulse to somehow wash and disinfect the boy. He had already become contaminated by this planet—by the Grooks. "It's mostly because of you that I am concerned about leaving," Morten said. "These people are savages, primitive. They will never rise above the level at which they are now. If you should stay you would become like them."

"I already am—very much like them."

"No. You can still see. They are blind, and their sight can never be healed."

Arlee had been experimenting in the galley of the ship, testing native fruits and vegetables for toxicity, and inventing ways to prepare them. She looked up in surprise as Morten came in.

"You're early. Did the class finish so quickly today?"

"There wasn't any class." Morten told her of the failure, and of Werk's explanation. "I was completely wrong about them," he said. "I had believed they

118

could be lifted up by education and put on the road to civilization, but they appear to have no desire for it. They are content to be what they are."

"I wonder if that isn't true of all of us," said Arlee slowly. She had her back to him as she stirred a pot of ill-smelling soup on the stove. "You and I. Free. The Grooks. Do any of us want to change? Civilization comes slowly, if at all. Maybe you took it too fast, tried too hard. You should have let the writing on the leaves be just a foolish game to them. Eventually, maybe one of them would have seen the utility of it."

"When?"

"Tomorrow. A year—ten years from now. Maybe a grandchild of one of your students. Who knows? Didn't it come that slowly on Earth?"

"That's too slow for Free. What good would such a world do him?"

"Free!" Arlee said angrily. "You think you can make him whatever you want. You just can't ever let go. You're like an artist with a piece of clay that is lumpy and won't stick together. You keep trying to put something together no matter how many times it falls apart."

"You're quite right," said Morten. "I will keep trying to put something together as long as I live. At least you should now be happy that I am going to give my full attention to the beacon and try to put something together out of it—no matter how many times it falls apart."

"I am glad—for that," said Arlee. "And I'm sorry I became angry, too. But I can't help being angry that you should have given up your whole life for *him*.

119

You have the best part of your career years ahead of you, years of research and discovery, and you refuse your duty to them. If you can repair the beacon and call for help why not leave Free right here? He loves these people; he has told me so. And they almost worship him."

"That would be worse than the euthanasia you wanted when he was an infant. No, I will continue trying to put him together also—no matter how many times my efforts fall apart.

"Because he *is* my son."

He returned in earnest to the task of analyzing the damage and attempting repair of the beacon. Although he had previously announced the impossibility of it he attacked the problem now with a new desperation. It was a necessity. It demanded his utmost effort and he was ready to give it now in a way he had not been committed before.

Free's salvation depended on getting him away from the primitiveness of this world to one where a degree of civilization flourished. That was the whole purpose of their coming, the whole object of his sacrifice. And now, as he looked out the port above the workbench, that sacrifice seemed of enormous proportions. He longed for the life of the laboratory, the conferences with his colleagues, the exhilaration of performing genetic miracles in his daily routine. He thought of the Grooks with repulsion now. He had almost exchanged all that to tutor a tribe of unwilling savages.

The beacon had been inoperative before the flight. It had suffered additional damage in the crash landing. As if he were dissecting a gene structure under the electron microscope he carefully disassembled the damaged structure of the beacon microcircuit by microcircuit. He was not skilled in electronics and mechanics because he had never taken the time. But these things were far less complex than gene combinations and molecular chemistry, which were his daily experience. He found it not too impossible to understand with the aid of a few textbooks which were part of the massive library he had included in their cargo.

It was time-consuming. Days passed and weeks. Morten detected a seasonal change appearing in the forest growth around them. And the temperature records, which Free kept meticulously, showed a slow drop in temperature. They had apparently landed in the middle of the planet's summer. Some rough calculations, based on the sun's elevation in the sky, showed there must be a seasonal variation not unlike that of Earth.

The effort on the beacon consumed all of Morten's time. He spent at least fourteen hours of each day at the workbench. Free took care of all the hunting and food gathering. Arlee prepared their meals now outside the ship, over a wood fire to conserve the energy of the ship.

Free spent all of his remaining time in the company of Werk and others of the Grooks. Morten disapproved of this close association, but he knew, too, that forbidding it would only leave Free restless and aggravate the seed of rebellion existing in the boy. He devised projects to keep Free busy. Projects that made some use of the boy's thin knowledge acquired in school.

He kept daily weather records of temperature and

humidity and wind movement, and measures of the not infrequent rain that fell. Morten gave him projects of measuring the sun's traverse of the sky and its daily variation of angle to plot a segment of the orbit of the planet and determine its inclination. He set him to gathering specimens of plants and preserving them with the Grook names that Werk gave him. And here the paucity of the Grook vocabulary was again apparent. The Grooks had named only a few plants. The rest were lumped under *echling*. Morten set Free to the task of dissecting plants and attempting to determine family trees.

As a full season passed and the half of another, Morten began to feel hope of salvaging the beacon. He understood how it worked. He knew where the areas of damage existed. The problem lay in replacing components irreparably damaged.

For most of these he found it possible to cannibalize other electronic circuits of the ship. Control circuits—that would never be needed again—yielded many items. Monitoring circuits, that no longer had anything to monitor. He withheld dismantling the navigational computer built into the pilot's console, for it was invaluable in solving other problems that arose. For most areas he found substitute components. For some others he had to devise ways of elimination. This consumed much time.

With the passage of another season, however, he was finished. The beacon was completed, tested, and put into working condition. A sun screen had been erected to provide sufficient power for its indefinite operation.

Arlee was ecstatic—and in tears with the happiness

of relief. "Now we can get off this forsaken world!" she exclaimed.

"Provided someone picks up our call and acts upon it," said Morten.

"They will! I know we'll be heard. I feel as if someone is on the way to us already. But this deserves a celebration. We should have a party."

"I'm afraid we have nothing left with which to drink a toast. The Grooks have some fermented jungle juice that would make a good metal polish, but there's nothing else."

"We don't need to drink a toast. Let's just be happy now that we've got a chance to get away," said Arlee fervently.

Morten caught a glimpse of movement in the passageway outside. He heard footsteps on the companionway. "I don't think Free is very happy about this. He's going to be grieved to leave the Grooks."

"Oh, don't spoil it. Please don't spoil it," Arlee begged.

As night came on they sat before the panels and watched the tiny glowing lights that showed the equipment was working. They watched the spools winding and rewinding the tape on which their distress message had been recorded, giving details of themselves and the location of the planet. The message would roll out constantly every minute of the day and night—as long as the equipment held out.

Or until a rescue ship arrived to pick them up.

They retired late, almost unable to leave the beacon as it hummed faintly in its task of notifying the universe that Morten Bradwell and his wife and his son were marooned on an unnamed planet. It was as if they expected the automatic alarm to sound at once, notifying them of an answering call.

They slept for a time, but Morten was awakened during the night by a howling that seemed to come through the sides of the ship and pervade the entire space around him. It took a moment to realize it was just the wind whining around the curve of the ship's upright column. But that was strange in itself. There had never been such a wind since their landing almost a year ago.

Morten got up and went to the port. He could hear the wind more plainly now, and he could see the trees bending before it in the faint dimness outside. He flashed on the exterior lights he had rigged for emergency use. In the glaring brilliance the wind was now seen to be whipping the trees in violence and beating the waters of the lake to waves that poured angrily up the shore.

The roof of the little schoolroom was already gone. The bare poles stuck upright in the ground like some archeological remains of a forgotten culture.

Behind him, Free padded on bare feet into the compartment. He looked past his father into the night. Morten moved aside and Free pressed his face against the port. "It's the night of the *baru*," he said solemnly.

"The night of the what——?"

"The *baru*. You wouldn't know. It's something the Grooks know about. They told me."

"Told you what? What is the *baru*?"

"It lives in the lake. It's some kind of living creature. The Grooks call it a devil. It comes out of the water on a night of fierce storm like this. It happens only once in many, many years. The Grooks say

124

the churning of the waves awakens it, and it comes out on the land and destroys villages and people."

"Can't they kill it—if there *is* such a creature as you describe?"

"They don't dare kill it. That would put them under its evil spell forever. But they drive it back to the water sometimes to protect a village. They shoot arrows with something on the tips."

"When did they last see it?"

"No one has seen it."

Morten laughed. "Then how do they know about it? How do they know what to do when it comes?"

"They say only their grandfathers have seen it—the grandfathers of the oldest Grooks alive. But it's real enough to them, and they pass down the secret of what to do about it from one generation to the next. They are always prepared. But they pray they may never have to attack it. There is always the danger that the poison they use may kill instead of just put the *baru* to sleep back in the water. They tell of one village that did kill the *baru* one time. Its people died horribly, withering away and dying in slow agony."

"Well, if *they* killed it, how is it that the *baru* might come again?"

"There is always one to take the place of one that is killed. The *baru is* immortal, they say. I don't understand it, but that is what they believe."

"The *baru* is immortal, but they fear to kill it—that's the kind of thinking you find among the Grooks!" Morten looked at his son with fondness and distress. "And do you want to live with a people who believe such incomprehensible things?"

"Oh, yes—these are little things. The big things are all those I do understand about them—and what they understand about me. The *baru* is just a little thing. I won't worry about that."

Morten turned back to the scene outside. In the light he saw flying pieces of debris lifted from the beach and out of the forest. The hull of the ship clanged with their impact. The beach sand whirled up in abrasive sheets that cut through the night.

"We had better go back to bed and try to get some sleep. It's a wild night out there." Morten paused and looked up, his feet planted a distance apart on the metal decking. A faint swaying moved the entire ship. "A little more of that, and we could go over," he said. "I hope it isn't a real hurricane building out there."

"I want to stay," said Free. "I want to watch for the *baru*."

"You don't really believe there is such a thing, do you?"

"Something—there must be something. They wouldn't make up a story like that. It has to be based on something. Maybe we can see whatever it is."

"I think the chance is zero, but call me if you see anything. I've got to get some sleep. This last week of work on the beacon has been a rough one."

He returned to the cabin, but slept little. Arlee was awake, too. He told her what Free had said about the Grooks and the *baru*.

"It's the kind of savage superstition you would expect," she said. "Are you surprised that Free believes it?"

126

He didn't want to argue with her in the fatigue of the night.

He must have dozed, he thought, because he couldn't remember the moments immediately before. He was just suddenly conscious of Free's hand on his shoulder, shaking him, and his voice, full of excitement, in his ear.

"Wake up, Dad! It's here—something's here. Come and see it."

"What's here?"

"The *baru,* maybe—or whatever the Grooks call *baru.* There's something out there!"

Morten slipped quickly into a robe and followed Free up the companionway. Arlee wakened, too, and he called back that he would be only a few minutes.

Free had turned on the exterior lights again. They illuminated the cleared area about the ship. But further toward the beach the night shadows continued dim.

As Free pointed excitedly, Morten saw something in those shadows. It was no more than a gray shape, but it moved.

"There *is* something out there," he agreed.

There was more than one. Three—four of the shadowy things moved. They seemed cylindrical, like massive gray serpents of enormous girth. But they tapered to probing tips that scratched and explored the sands leading from the beach.

The wind had diminished considerably now. Tree branches still whipped and lurched, but they did not bow as if in death to the steady crushing blast that had beat them earlier.

Then Free caught sight of another scene through

127

another port. He called out to Morten. "Look, Dad —the Grook villages—"

Morten glanced in the direction and saw a half dozen pinpoints of light far down the beach and across the span of the lake. The native villages were lit by fires that flickered and thrust their light before the wind like some warning beacons.

"Do you know what it means?" said Morten.

"No. Just that the Grooks are awake and outside. They know this is the night of the *baru*. They must know that he is coming, that he is out of the lake now."

Morten made a growling noise of disgust in his throat and turned back to the other port where the moving creatures advanced toward the clearing. He gave a gasp as he saw the scene again.

"What is it, Dad?"

The writhing cylinders had advanced a considerable distance now. The tips of them were within the edge of illumination from the lights. They looked like something he had seen in ancient pictures of sea creatures.

The tips twisted, turning, seeking, touching each other, then flinging out again for something new. They seemed like snakes. Enormous, blind snakes, Morten thought.

He watched as they advanced into the circle of light. Their diameter increased as more of their length was revealed. Already they were almost a meter thick. He counted six of them.

And then an enormous shadow, far larger than anything seen so far, became apparent just out of range of the lights. It seemed to surge and quiver with the movement of the probing columns. Morten realized suddenly what it was. The writhing probes were not a half dozen individual creatures. They were tentacles, extensions, of a single animal. This dimly seen shadow was the central body.

Morten strained his eyes to see it. He turned off the lights once to try to distinguish the faint outline, but was left blinded in the darkness. He turned on the lights again and waited for the central body to move closer.

It was at least six meters in height, roughly globular in shape. The massive tentacles eased it forward slowly while they continued their incessant probing in all directions. At the edge of the clearing one of the tentacles wrapped itself around a twenty-centimeter tree trunk. The tentacle tightened and pulled.

With little apparent change in the creature's motion, the tentacle slowly bent the trunk of the tree until it uprooted and fell with a slow, graceful motion. The tentacle dragged it a meter or two and released it. The awesome power of those arms of gray, rubbery flesh chilled Morton.

"It's coming toward the ship," said Free. "What do you think it will do?"

"I don't know, but I don't think we should wait to find out. Get a pair of the boron guns and let's go up to the parapet."

Free nodded and obeyed. He brought two of the powerful guns while Morten opened the hatches in the nose. They formed work platforms outside the ship, which they called the parapet. "We'll each take one," said Morten. "Start firing as soon as you're in place."

They climbed the short ladders to the outside and

stood on the platforms, looking down at the writhing beast whose central body was now well within the circle of light. The enormous size of the creature was fully revealed. If its tentacles were stretched to their limit they would span the entire clearing.

Morten wondered for a moment whether it would be better to simply allow the creature to return to the lake—if that's what it intended to do—rather than risk antagonizing it with shots. But it seemed to have no intention of going back to the water now, and two or three charges from the boron guns ought to be all it would take to destroy the monster.

Its present goal seemed to be the ship. Even as Morten watched, the probing tip of the nearest tentacle touched the hull. It snaked around, coiling over the smooth surface as it had the tree it uprooted moments before.

The ship trembled from the touch and the tug of those tons of flesh. It would be a simple matter for the creature to topple the ship to the ground, destroying the work of months that Morten had put into the repair of the beacon.

"Fire!" he cried out to Free. "It's going to try to tip us over!"

XI

Morten aimed for the center of the body and pressed the button. The charge burst from the tube with a small speck of light that flared against the soft flesh and was swallowed by it.

There appeared to be no effect. From his side, Free pressed the firing button on his rifle, and Morten aimed and fired again and again.

A score of missiles entered the soft flesh with no apparent effect. Morten stared down at the creature in disbelief. The charges were designed to collapse the synapses of any cellular organism.

The tentacle tightened its grasp of the ship's hull and with a swift burst of motion encircled it completely. The central body was almost directly below Morten. Something that seemed to resemble a mouth or a deeply set eye flicked open and shut with a puckering motion in the center of the body. Morten fired into it. A dozen bursts. The puckering motion intensified. Otherwise, there was no effect.

The ship trembled with the crushing movement of

the tentacle. Another began its encircling motion higher up. It looked as if the creature intended climbing the column of the ship's hull. If it put the entire weight of those tons of flesh on one side the ship would certainly topple.

"The guns won't do it, Dad!" Free cried out from his parapet. "We can't kill it with these!"

It was incredible, but it was true. The boron guns had no effect whatever—and a single shot was capable of killing anything living—on Earth. Morten raised the gun once more and fired two score bursts into the mass, without effect. Its body and cellular structure must be something entirely different from anything men had encountered before.

Morten returned to the pilot's compartment and called Free to join him. Arlee was there when they dropped down from the ladders.

"I heard you," she said. "I see it out there. Can it hurt us in here, even if you can't kill it?"

Morten showed her it was beginning an attempt to climb the hull. "It will topple us,' 'he said. "We'd best go down to the bottom level and prepare to rush out if the ship begins to go over."

"We can't, Dad," said Free. "I saw—the tentacles cover the lower hatch. We can't open it."

Morten felt the floor beneath their feet shake again. "There's a baggage hatch on the level above ground level. We could open it and drop to the ground."

"We'd be right on top of the tentacles," said Arlee.

"Free says the Grooks have something powerful enough to control the creature. If only we knew the nature of the substance we might be able to concoct it from our stores. Do you have any idea what they use, Free?"

Free had taken a seat at the pilot's console, and now he was rigid, staring ahead as if not seeing anything in the room.

"Free!" Morten shook him to command his attention. Free raised a hand to appeal for a moment's respite. Something about the gesture made Morten retreat. He waited, not knowing for what, while Free continued staring.

At last he stirred. "That was Werk," he said. "He talked to me the way they can talk to each other. I have never done it before, but Werk wanted me so desperately that he came through."

"What did he say?"

"They know the *baru* is out of the water and threatening us. He asked about us, and I told him our guns wouldn't touch it and it was about to crush our ship."

"Did you ask if they could help?"

"That's why Werk was trying to reach me. They thought we might need help. It is against all their principles to attack the *baru* where the *baru* has not come to them. But he thinks they will do it for me."

"Why you?"

Free spread his hands in a gesture of ignorance. "They like me, I think they like me very much."

Something about the admission chilled Morten, but he did not know what it was. He said, "How will they help? We need it right now. If the *baru* should take a notion, he could tip us over right now."

"There is a group armed to meet the *baru*. They have been hiding in the forest by the lake since the beginning of the storm. They are ready for the *baru*. They will come to us."

"Ask Werk how long it will we be. Tell him we can't hold out much longer. We'll have to jump and try to make a run for it."

Free shook his head. "I can't any more. I'm not like the Grooks. I need to practice a lot before I get like them."

Morten crossed to the port and looked in the direction of the darkened jungle from which he supposed the Grooks would come. There was nothing to be seen in the darkness.

The wind was rising again. They heard its faint cry against the hull and felt the vibration. Rain began to fall now in sheets that were swept and beaten by the wind. Morten wondered if this weather change would affect the *baru*. He supposed not.

More important, what would it do to the Grooks out in the forest? Would they continue in the face of such storm? Why would they do so if the *baru* was offering them no threat? He pondered the statement Free had made: "They like me. I think they like me very much."

Why? he wondered. Why should it be so?

A quarter of an hour passed. They could hear the creaking of stressed metal as the *baru*'s coiled grip tightened on the hull. The floor tilted and swayed momentarily as the grip of the giant tentacle increased and then relaxed. Morten wondered how far away the Grooks were. And even as he did so he wondered at his ready acceptance of the story that the Grooks could conquer the *baru*. That was ridiculous, his reason told him. If the boron gun's repeated charges had no effect, certainly no potion delivered by bow and arrow would have. And it had never even been tried within the memory of any living Grook. It was idiocy to rely on them.

"Let's get ready to leave the ship," said Morten.

"They'll be here," exclaimed Free. "Give them a chance!"

"We're the ones risking the chance," said Morten. "We'll be crushed if the hull collapses or tips us over. Let's get the baggage hatch open."

Arlee stood up, ready to go. She took a long look at the still humming beacon and its whirling tape. "If only there had been enough time—" she said.

Morten left the pilot's compartment with Arlee, Free following reluctantly. Morten admitted he didn't know what they would do out in the storm, but the urgency was increasing by the minute. The creaking of the hull under the crushing force of the *baru* was almost continuous now. The shaking of the floors shook objects in their cabinets. The hull could go over at any moment.

They stopped in the cabins long enough to grab rain gear. They could come back for other things that would not be damaged by the toppling of the ship. At the baggage level Morten undogged the small hatch and flung it open to the storm. Rain slashed in at them and forced them back from the opening.

"We can't go out in that!" Arlee cried.

Below them the thick trunks of two tentacles lay coiled about the hull. The gray, rubbery flesh glistened under the glare of the lights. It rippled and quivered with the tightening of the powerful muscles in the coil. Rainwater collected in puddles between the curve of the ship and the curve of the fleshy extrusion. Thick lipped cups for suction opened and closed like a million nauseating mouths against the metal wall.

Morten was trying to estimate the force necessary to jump clear of the tentacles. He wondered if the creature might be able to sense their presence near its extensions. If so, those mighty arms would swing out and crush them as they jumped.

There might be greater safety in staying with the ship, after all, he thought. If they secured themselves on the lowest level they would not suffer much from the ship's overturning. And perhaps that would satisfy the creature. It might not be compelled to crush the ship completely.

Then, abruptly, Free gestured to the forest far beyond the circle of light. He held up a finger in caution and turned his head to listen. "Hear it?" he cried. "The Grooks are out there!"

Morten turned his head. He heard nothing but the dense sloshing of the rain. "I don't hear anything."

"There it comes again!"

Morten heard it then. A long, wailing cry of human voices raised as if in torment. It was a symphony of human sound that melted into the sound of the storm. A cry like the wind. A cry like the despair of death.

"It's their song to the *baru*," said Free. "They are pleading for the *baru*'s forgiveness for what they must do."

Morten listened to the faint wail. He could almost sense the meaning Free gave the sound. It was like an acknowledgement of the *baru*'s kingship over the dark

136

things of the universe, a tribute to its evil power.

"What will they do?" Morten felt only half certain he had heard anything at all. But Arlee nodded. "I hear it, too."

"They will come up and shoot their painted arrows into the *baru* to drive it back to the water. They must be very careful not to kill it."

The singing was plainly audible now. The wind shifted and carried the sound sharply to their ears. Morten felt cold, but he didn't know whether it was the wailing symphony or the cold slash of wind-driven rain that caused it.

Below them, the flesh of the *baru* suddenly trembled like the flesh of a heart in fibrillation. Uncontrolled spasms swept through it, almost in time with the rise and fall of the Grook voices. And as it quivered, the hold of the tentacles on the metal wall of the ship slackened perceptibly.

"All right," said Morten decisively. "We'll go with the Grooks."

They backed away as he closed the hatch and dogged the fasteners once more. They returned to the pilot's compartment and the observation ports.

They looked down once more upon the central body of the *baru*. The orifice in the top of it was pulsing and puckering violently. Morten thought he saw a red glow at its center, as if a hidden eye had become inflamed. The whole body quivered as the crescendo chant of the Grook voices washed over it.

The tentacles were mostly quiet now. Instead of their restless probing they withdrew and contracted. The two that were wrapped around the ship slowly retracted and drew close to the body. The entire creature slewed around as if to face the attackers, although there was nothing by which the Earthmen could distinguish one side of the creature from the other.

Without warning, the column of Grooks appeared at the edge of the clearing. Their singing ceased. They stood erect, lined up in a row facing the *baru,* waiting in the slashing rain as if for some sign to begin the attack.

With binoculars, Morten examined the tense, desperate figures. Water streamed down their faces and the naked torsos. Their tribal dress of brief skirts was drenched. This was a venture that would be related to their sons and to the sons of their sons for generations to come.

Slowly, one man from near the end of the line stepped out with a measured tread, advancing almost to the edge of a coiled tentacle. The *baru* could have lashed out and crushed the Grook instantly, but it did not.

A curious quietness seemed to have come over the monster. The Grook raised his arms and began intoning a chant, but he was too far away for those in the ship to hear the words.

"He's praying to the *baru,*" said Free. "He's asking pardon again for what they must do. He's asking the *baru* not to send devils and evil upon the Grook folk. This is what Werk told me they would do."

The man finished his intonation and lowered his hands. Then, with great deliberation he unslung his bow and fitted an arrow. He drew it back and aimed for the center of the great, globular body. A tremor swept through the gray mass, and the tips of the tentacles began their restless weaving again.

The Grook released the arrow. It penetrated half the length of its shaft. The *baru* recoiled, its forward half-circle of tentacles rising and flailing the air as if some vital nerve had been pierced. Morten thought he almost sensed a cry of pain from the creature, but was sure there had been no audible sound.

The Grook remained motionless where he stood.

"Why doesn't the fool run?" Morten cried. His hands clenched the rim of the port as if he would cry out a warning to the man below. Free offered no answer, but his own face was white as he watched—as if knowing what was to come.

The tentacles thrashed. Then two of them whipped down and swept the Grook from his feet. He was carried high into the air, his screams shrieking through the wind momentarily until they were cut off by the crushing force that held him.

The Grook was crushed close to the center of the *baru*'s mass. The tentacles hung there for a moment. When they moved away the body of the Grook was not to be seen. There must have been a mouth, Morten thought in numb disbelief, but they had seen nothing.

"It had to be that way," said Free hoarsely. "They give one man to the *Baru*. It won't be angry then and take vengeance on their villages."

As if the disappearance of their companion were the signal, the Grook bowmen raised their weapons in unison and loosed their arrows. The points pierced the *baru*'s soft flesh in a score of places. The gray skin contracted and rippled in violent waves that could be only waves of agony, Morten thought. The tentacles thrashed as the control synapses were suddenly tangled. One tentacle slapped the ship in a massive blow that rocked it on its base and sent tremors of sound across the clearing.

Then the tentacles slid around the cylinder of the hull and crushed with fury. The metal screamed and twisted.

"It's crushing the ship again!" Arlee cried.

Morten spread his feet to retain balance on the quaking deck. "Let's get below! The bottom level. If it goes over with that violence—"

"Wait!" Free was straining to see through the shifting port.

"What is it?" Morten demanded.

"See," said Free. "The Grooks are going to shoot again."

Morten glanced out. The natives raised their arrows once more in formation and let fly. "What difference does it make?" said Morten. "Their arrows can't drive it off any more than our boron guns can."

Free watched a third volley of arrows with a kind of horror on his face. "You don't understand, Dad! They're killing the *baru!* They're killing the *baru* for me—for us."

The shaking of the deck had ceased. Morten saw the gray coils retract again. Then the *baru* turned with infinite slowness and began a half rolling, half sliding motion in the direction of the lake, propelled by the wild, slow flinging of its arms.

The Grook bowmen advanced farther and stood between the ship and the *baru*. They raised their arrows, but there was no need to shoot again.

"They've never killed the baru before," Free whispered. "They did it—to keep the *baru* from killing —us."

Morten remembered how Free had used the word "me" the first time. He didn't understand. Free seemed to know something he did not.

"Maybe they've decided there's been enough destruction by the monster; it's time they got rid of it," Morten said to him.

"Werk said they would not kill it. They were not supposed to."

"It doesn't mean anything to us, whether they kill it or not. Or do you think it does—?"

"I think it does," said Free slowly. "It means they've decided something about us. I'm not sure what it is."

Morten stared at Free as if seeing some danger settling over him. But there was nothing tangible. All the night terrors should be headed toward the dark waters of the lake with the dying *baru*, but something remained. Something far less tangible, but as equally threatening in its own way.

XII

The storm-free sky the next morning gave no sign of the turmoil and destruction of the night. The few ragged remnants of clouds were fast disappearing. About the ship, the clearing was strewn with wind-whipped debris. Huge limbs, that belonged to no nearby tree, were jammed against the bare poles of the schoolroom.

They went to the beach, half-hopeful, half-fearful of what they might see. Nothing was apparent.

"It was a nightmare," said Arlee. "We only dreamed it."

"Here's the trail," said Free.

It looked as if a gigantic sack had been dragged along the ground from the clearing to the beach. Morten raised the binoculars to his eyes and scanned the surface of the lake. Abruptly, he stiffened and remained watching in one direction. Arlee and Free strained to see in the direction of the binoculars. A faint, indefinable smudge appeared far out.

"What is it Dad?" Free asked.

Morten lowered the glasses slowly and handed them to Free. The boy looked toward the smudge. In the glasses it became a black, irregular disk, slightly raised in the center, floating on the water. "It's the *baru*, isn't it?" said Free.

"I suppose so," said Morten. "If we only had a boat—I'd like to get a specimen of its tissue and try to find out why a boron gun won't touch it, but a simple, poisoned arrow will. Do the Grooks have boats?"

"There are some way over on the other side."

"It would be too badly decomposed by the time we could reach it."

Free handed the glasses to his mother.

"I'll take your word for it. I've seen enough of *baru* to last a lifetime," said Arlee.

Free raised the glasses again and continued to stare. "They shouldn't have killed it," he murmured. "It will be upon their heads for generations to come. And they did it—for us."

They returned to the clearing, and Morten began cleaning up some of the debris.

"Why do that?" said Arlee. "We won't need the area."

"We may need it for a long time. Anyway, we want to have a tidy place when and if any rescuers arrive. Besides, it's something to do." Morten glanced in Free's direction. Arlee nodded agreement.

They resumed their routine of housekeeping, food gathering, maintaining the camp—and tending the beacon. Free stayed close for a day or two, then resumed his wandering off among the Grooks. Werk did not show up.

Morten and Arlee listened frequently to space calls caught by the beacon receiver. They sometimes heard ships exchanging traffic with one another and with home bases. But none of these ships appeared to have picked up the signal from the beacon. Morten began to wonder if it were transmitting properly after all. But he checked and rechecked and could find no malfunction in it. He began to think there might be some unknown magnetic field about the planet which sucked back all electromagnetic radiation. And he knew his sanity must be slipping when he conceived such nonsensical thoughts.

He longed for his past dream of educating the Grooks, for then he could see the possibility of Free remaining with them. As it was, they continued to exhibit a savage indifference to any but their own ways It was curious, Morten thought, that they should have the one outstanding ability of telepathic communication. He looked for other concommitant gifts, but there were none. This one stood out alone. It was the only quality that atoned for their savagery and rejection of any deeper knowledge of the world about them.

Free spent increasing amounts of time with them. In addition to Werk, he had made a wide range of friends among the Grooks throughout the villages up and down the lake shore. He slept less and less frequently in the ship, spending many nights with his savage friends.

Morten feared the results. When it came time for Free to leave—if it ever did—the pain would be great in severing the attachment that was growing between Free and the Grooks.

But he didn't know if it would ever happen.

Then, one night a month after the night of the *baru*, the miracle happened. The beacon alarm sounded to indicate the signal have been received and that a response was coming in.

Morten leaped from the bed and ran up the companionway to the pilot's chamber to answer the call and shut off the alarm. Arlee was right behind him.

His hands trembled as he pressed the button to transmit a reply. He spoke into the microphone. "Morten Bradwell calling Cephon II. Morten Bradwell calling —"

He repeated the call and listened. In a moment the hyperspace transmission was answered. "Patrol cruiser Cephon II calling Morten Bradwell. This is Commander Reynolds. We picked up your distress call and have your coordinates. We are heading in your direction immediately. Please state your condition and circumstances."

Morten could scarcely control his voice as he replied to the patrol ship. Arlee stood beside his chair, trembling as he was at the prospect of rescue after so long an exile. Morten gave a brief statement of their situation and their need for pickup. "We are in good health. No injuries or illness to be cared for. Our only need is for transportation to a point where passage to our destination can be obtained. How long will your arrival take?"

"Twelve days, Earth normal. We read you. Your condition is good. No present emergency. You require only transportation. Keep your beacon on. We will use it for homing in case your coordinates are off. We will check with you daily at this hour until arrival."

The voice cut off and Morten slumped in an exhaustion of relief. He had not known he was sprung to such tenseness over the fact of their exile.

He looked up finally to Arlee and embraced her, his eyes wet with tears, as hers were. "We can go home now," he said.

"Home or Randor?" said Arlee.

"I wonder. I wonder what I do mean. There is still Free—we have to go to Randor, for his sake. But I would prefer home. I truly would."

"Then maybe that's where we'll go—in the end," said Arlee gently.

They returned to bed. Free was not aboard ship. He had been with the Grooks for several days. Morten wondered how he would take the news that they were going to be rescued. How would he take leave of the Grooks to whom he had become so attached?

Free returned the following morning. Morten met him in the clearing beside the cooking-eating area they had built. They sat down together on the rough bench by the table. "The Grooks have asked me to live with them all the time," said Free. "Would you mind very much if I did that, Dad? I would come back to see you and Mom real often, of course—"

Morten hesitated a long time, until Free finally looked at him and said, "Did you hear what I said, Dad?"

Morten nodded. "I heard. I have something to tell you, too. We had a response to the beacon last night. A patrol ship is on its way to pick us up."

Free's face was agonized. "When? How soon will they be here?"

"A little less than two weeks."

"And I must go back?"

"You must go back, Free. Not back to Earth, where things were so difficult for you, but on to Randor, where we will find people who will understand you and accept you."

"I have already found people who understand me and accept me!" Free exclaimed. "This is my world, Dad. I am Star Prince here. You can't make me leave now that I've found it again."

"You were born on Earth," said Morten gently. "Don't you understand, Free? You have never been here before. Our minds do strange things for us at times. They make us think things happened that never did really happen. You couldn't have known the Grooks at any previous time. It's one of those tricks the mind plays on us sometimes."

"It's no trick. This is my world. I am the Star Prince here. The Grooks know it, too. Why do you think they killed the *baru*? They risked all the evil the *baru* might bring upon them, because they believed the Star Prince could more than overcome all the evil of the *baru*. They risked their whole future, their whole people, for me."

"It will die away," said Morten desperately. "On Randor you will learn and grow. If you stayed here you would wither and become more savage and child-like every year—just like the Grooks."

"I want to be like the Grooks. I want to be just like them and like nobody else!"

His strength chilled Morten. "You will forget them

in time. There will be so many new things to do and learn on Randor that you will wonder how you could ever have tolerated the Grooks."

Free exhaled deeply and bitterly. He said finally, "I must go, then?"

"It's for your own good. I'm leaving Earth and giving up the things I have there in order to give you this opportunity. If I didn't think it was worth it I wouldn't do that, would I?"

Free shook his head, then got up slowly and walked away, down to the shore of the lake and on toward the villages of the Grooks. Morten wondered if he ought to hold Free by force now, lock him in the ship until the patrol arrived. Was there a chance the boy would rebel and run away to the Grooks and refuse to leave? He didn't believe so, but he wondered if he ought to take the chance.

Free returned, however, that night. He slept in his cabin in the ship and stayed close by for a couple of days. His face and manner were brooding and quiet. He had little to say, but he seemed resigned to obedience to Morten's decision.

The daily checks with the patrol ship continued. There were no problems. The ship was on course and on schedule. It was routine to the patrol, although it was a monumental event to the Bradwells.

Two days before the scheduled arrival of the ship they began packing their possessions and the specimens from the planet which they desired to take with them. Free joined the activitity without protest. He had a sizable collection of artifacts the Grooks had given him. A bow and some arrows. Primitive tools. Dress. Pieces of art and figurines of gods of the forest and sky. The leaf on which Werk had written: Don't go away, Free.

They slept aboard ship that night, aware that it was next to the last night there. It was difficult, but they slept at last, exhausted by their anticipation, pleasurable for Morten and Arlee, painful for Free.

Sometime during the middle of the night they were awakened by sounds within the ship. Morten sat up. The sounds continued, and a flicker of light appeared in the passageway outside the door. He grasped his robe and strode to the doorway.

A figure stepped behind him and clutched him in a grasp that pinned his arms to his sides. He struggled furiously and failed to break the hold. By the light of a flickering torch carried up the companionway Morten saw he was surrounded by Grooks. They filled the ship and were swarming into Free's cabin. A trio of them went behind Morten and returned with Arlee's struggling figure.

Morten ceased his struggles and looked about at the captors. Some of them he recognized. Some had been in his long-ago class. "Why have you come here?" he demanded in their own language.

Then, from the outer edge of the crowd, Werk came forward. "We cannot let you go, Mr. Bradwell. We cannot let you take the Star Prince."

"You're insane! This crazy story of Free's has you all deluded. He is from Earth, a planet so far from here you could never understand the distance. We leave tomorrow for our own worlds and our own people."

"We are Free's own people," said Werk obstinately," and this is his world. We have waited lifetimes for his coming. The fathers of our oldest fathers spoke of the coming of the Star Prince and we will not let you take him from us." Werk came close, his eyes hard and older—far older—now as he looked into Morten's.

"For the Star Prince we have killed the *baru*. The terror of the sky will fall upon us, the fiery mouths of the ground will open beneath us. Our mothers and our wives and our daughters will wither and die, and our men will crawl upon the ground in weakness. This the *baru* will bring upon us, and only the Star Prince can be our guide and protector now. You cannot take him from us. He knows his life and destiny is here with us, his people."

"Then let his mother and me go," said Morten. "There is nothing for us here."

Werk shook his head. "We have considered that. But we know it is in your heart to return with many men to take the Star Prince from us. We will be kind and treat you always as one of us, but we will not let you go."

"What do you intend to do?"

"We will not harm you. We will take you to a place where the men from the stars cannot find you."

Morten looked about quickly. There was no way of freeing himself from the grasp of the Grooks. They surrounded him and Arlee on all sides. And Arlee was crying now as she understood the full impact of the Grook's words.

Free, near the wall of the lounge, was not being watched by the natives. He was white faced and tense. Morten regarded him bitterly. This was the result of his going to the Grooks that morning after Morten

151

had told him of the patrol ship. But maybe he was not wholly turned against his parents—

"Free!" Morten called. "The pilot's compartment. The boron guns!"

Free was by the companionway. He could flee up the steps and have the guns in his hands. They had not been moved since they were used against the *baru*.

But Free remained rigid, unmoving. "These are my friends. These are my people." He repeated the words as if they were a recording.

"*We* are your people!" Morten cried. He would not have believed it. To prevent his parents from leaving, Free had brought the Grooks here. He had undogged the hatch below to let them in.

Free avoided his glance.

"Allow us to get dressed and take those things that are necessary," Morten said.

"Of course." Werk nodded to those who barred the way. "We will help you carry the things that you need, but you can return here as soon as the other men have come and gone."

While they were dressing in the cabin they heard the sudden smashing of glass and crash of metal upon metal. It came from above. They stared, motionless, at the closed door. Then Arlee gasped in agony. "The beacon! Morten—they're smashing the beacon."

He knew it was true. Free had shown Werk how they had called for rescuers, and now the Grooks were smashing the beacon so they would be forever cut off. He wondered if Free were helping to smash the equipment, too.

Arlee whirled on Morten. "Your precious Free has just destroyed the rest of our lives! Maybe you know

152

now why there is provision to euthanize Retards before they mature!"

Morton wrote a note of explanation, hoping the patrol officers would find it. He wished he could hide it, but he had to leave it where they would find it. On the dressing table.

They opened the door to go out. Werk came in and glanced about the room. His eye caught the writing on the table and he picked up the paper. Morten knew he could not read it, but he guessed. "No writing, Mr. Bradwell. We do not want the men from the stars searching our villages."

"At least one pupil understood," said Morten.

They went out into the night with the small packs they carried to tide them over until the patrol had gone. Morten carried the binoculars in the hope of seeing the patrol when it arrived, althought he had no idea what use this might be. The group stayed close to the shore of the lake as they began what seemed like an endless journey through the night.

At sunrise they stopped for food. They were served at one of the villages by which they passed. It was not the same kind of repulsive fare that Morten had been given previously. It was a plate of meat and vegetables that was rather good, and Morten thanked their hosts of the village.

They continued on through the day in the same manner, stopping at midday and at evening. By nightfall they had almost rounded the curve of the lake and were approaching the shore directly opposite the ship and their camp.

"We'll stop here for the night," said Werk. "It is not much farther, but it would be best to arrive in

153

the morning." The Grook boy continued to be their contact, but he took instructions from an older gray-haired Grook who was the leader.

In the night, Free lay beside them, next to Morten. He couldn't sleep. "I didn't know they would do this, Dad," he said. "They promised they would only take me and let you go. I agreed because I wanted you to think they had forced me to stay, not that I was disobeying you and staying behind. It all went wrong. Everything went wrong." He was crying in his remorse.

Morten believed him. "It's all right, Free. You did what you thought was best to do." There was no use trying to sort out Free's tangled reasoning and misunderstandings. Morten didn't even want to speak of the smashing of the equipment aboard the ship. It was over, and they were trapped.

Arlee lay crying bitterly, too. Morten reached over and tried to comfort her, but she would not be comforted. The vast hopes built up during the weeks of work on the beacon had been shattered, and there was nothing to salvage. The patrol ship would land, the crew would be unable to find them and would finally leave again without them. The patrolmen would conclude some disaster had overtaken them since the last communication. But they would not search widely to find out. That was not their mission.

They slept finally for a short time before the sun rose and the Grooks were preparing to march again.

Their destination was the line of cliffs they had observed on the other side of the lake. The cliffs were pocked with caves of varying sizes, many of them large. The Grooks had made some of them livable with primitive furniture and fireplaces and storage pits.

The Grook captors led them to the largest and best furnished. "You will be provided everything you need," said Werk, "but you must not attempt to leave until you are told."

Standing in the entrance to the cave, Morten raised the binoculars to his eyes and focussed across the lake. The clearing and the ship were easily seen. "We shall be able to see the patrol when it arrives," he said. It should be only a few hours away, at most. This was the day the rescue ship was scheduled to arrive.

"As if that will be any comfort," said Arlee. And then, as if seeing Free for the first time, she turned upon him. "Keep out of my sight! We'll live all the rest of our lives on this miserable planet because of you. You betrayed us for those filthy degenerates that infest this place."

"Mom—"

"Arlee—" Morten interposed himself between them. "Free made a mistake. He trusted them and they betrayed him. There is nothing to be gained by reviling him."

She whirled away in silence and flung herself down on a rude couch by the wall of the cavern.

Morten sank to a chair opposite her, and Free sat far back in the darkened corner of the cave.

XIII

What have we come to? Morten thought. Surely the bright product of the generations of genetic engineering should have been able to do better than this. Arlee was consumed by a hatred of Free that would not let her go. And he, Morten, had been consumed by a dream that he could raise the poor creatures, the Grooks, to some semblance of civilization, and nothing in his experience or his inheritance had been able to tell him how to do it. He had been rejected by this primitive, ignorant tribe whose members would not even have been allowed to exist on Earth.

And he didn't know for certain whether he had been tricked and deceived by Free or whether the poor, simple Retard had been deceived by the Grooks. In the end it mattered little. The result was the same. The patrol would come. They would search the ship and look about the clearing. They would find no trace of the Bradwells and would wonder about the smashed beacon. And then they would go. Eventually they would file a final report detailing their failure to locate the missing family. And that wou'd be the end of it.

A trio of Grooks app ared and erected a woven grass screen over the entrance to the ca ern. "It is so you will not be seen by the men who come from the stars," they explained. "You must remain inside and not be seen or you will be shot with an arrow." This was said so matter-of-factly that Morten was convinced it was true.

They were given a midday meal and ate in silence. Morten tried to make talk, but his own depression outweighed every attempt to speak of any subject. The hope of rescue had been raised in him, too, where he had never believed it was going to be possible. Now, it was hard to abandon. Harder, because of what Free had done.

"How do they know so exactly when the patrol is coming?" Morten asked Free. "You must have told them."

"They read it out of my mind that men from the stars were coming to take us away—and when they were coming."

"They can't do that without your consent, can they?"

"I was sick and afraid. I had to let them know I was going. That was when I got the idea of having them kidnap me out of the ship, so you wouldn't know I was doing it myself. It would have worked all right if they hadn't gotten the idea you must be held, too."

It was his own fault, Morten thought. He had ignored the fact that Free was a Retard and must always be treated as one.

They returned to their isolated places in the cavern

to wait. Morten felt as anxious to hear the sound as if he were standing in the clearing outside his own ship, his eyes straining to the sky, waiting for that speck that would mean release at last.

They heard it then. Two sounds, really. The shrill, high-pitched whine of splitting air, and then the low thunder of braking engines. Morten rose and strode to the curtain over the mouth of the cave. He peered through the slots between the fibers and widened a place with his finger enough to see with the binoculars.

He saw it, high in the sky, the slim blue projectiles of the patrol with its silver markings. It dropped swiftly but gently, lowering itself to the clearing. It seemed so natural that the ship should be landing that Morten wondered how he could ever have doubted that it would come.

It settled slowly over the tops of the trees, and then down amidst them. With a fury of debris blown aside by its blast, the ship touched down a dozen meters from their own crippled vessel.

"May I see, Dad?" Free asked in apologetic voice for the glasses. Morten handed them over.

Three men alighted from the ship. They moved briskly and urgently to the courier with its wide open hatch and its total abandonment.

"Let me see now, son."

Free handed the glasses back. The men came quickly out of the ship and returned to their own vessel. Once more they came out.

They walked about then, as if in puzzlement that no one was there to meet them. If only Earthmen had the telepathic abilities of the ignorant, savage Grooks,

Morten thought. It was as if every cell of his being cried out in silent plea to the dismayed patrolmen.

One of them returned to the ship and came out with a horn. He spoke into it and his voice was amplified and carried across the waters of the lake. Morten heard him clearly: "Morten Bradwell, the patrol cruiser has landed. We are prepared to take you off. Come at once!"

Two of the patrolmen walked a little way down the beach while one remained as if on guard by their ship. The two did not go far. They were not going to make any kind of search on foot. Morten understood; it would have been utterly impractical to make a search. Undoubtedly, they were scanning the forest for a depth of some miles with electronic detectors. From the trace they had made of Morten's voice during his call for help they would have been able to spot him if their detectors reached him. But the distance across the lake put him out of range.

At fifteen minute intervals they repeated the vocal announcement. Each time, Arlee looked dully from Morten to Free, as if undecided now where the blame lay. Free returned and huddled in his corner at the back of the cavern, not able to endure the presence of the patrolmen longer.

Morten continued to watch as if by some tenuous power he could project his longing, his anxiety across the miles of water. As twilight came, the man repeated his announcement and added: "This is our last call. We will wait one half hour and then make our departure. Morten Bradwell, come to the clearing for lift-off within one half hour."

They had been there for six hours now. Morten

lowered the glasses and let them hang from the strap about his neck. He rubbed his eyes and turned away from the slit in the screen.

"Are they leaving?" said Arlee.

"Half hour. They said they would wait only that much longer. Do you want to look?"

"No. I don't want to have to remember the sight of our one chance of escape."

Morten glanced at the watch he still wore on his wrist. He watched the minutes tick off. You want to see?" he offered the glasses to Free once more. The boy shook his head.

At last he put the glasses to his own eyes again. The patrolmen had disappeared into their ship. The hatch was closed. He guessed they were watching on their screens until the very last minute for any sign of those they had come to rescue.

Abruptly, with a brief flurry of fire from its secondary engines the ship took off. Morten followed it as long as he could on its white trail into the sky. Then he could see it no more.

He turned back to the darkness of the cavern room. He could scarcely see the others now. He sat on the chair against the wall opposite Arlee.

After a long time she said, "What now?"

"I don't know. I suppose they'll let us go back to the ship, as they said they would. Do you know what they are going to do with us now, Free?"

"I don't know. I think they'll let you go. Werk hasn't told me."

Morten leaned back and rested his head against the stone wall. He closed his eyes. In his mind he saw the planet from the observation screen of the cruiser.

Its green, cloud-specked silhouette diminished slowly and vanished from sight. A great sob escaped him. He had never never known how much he had yearned for that departure. Even when he had been filled with hope that he could civilize the Grooks he had been deceiving himself, he thought. The prospect of lifetime exile on this world had always been a terror he had refused to admit to himself. Now it was reality and he could no longer hide from it.

The screen was jerked aside abruptly and a shadow stood there against the lighter shadow of the deepening night. It was Werk. "You are free to go." He could not see Morten in the cave darkness but he spoke in the direction he knew he must be. "You may leave as early in the morning as you like."

"Tonight," said Morten. "Is there any reason we cannot leave tonight?"

"No. But it is dark on the path. You should wait until morning."

"Tonight." It was as if he could not endure another moment's confinement in the cavern. "Come on, Arlee. Free."

Arlee was as anxious as he was, but Free did not move. "I have to stay. I'll be a day or two, and then I'll come."

Morten felt he didn't even care. Free's betrayal, even in all its innocent ignorance and stupidity, had made the prospect of living with him again a distasteful burden. The boy undoubtedly would live with the Grooks from now on. It just didn't matter any more.

He took Arlee's hand as they picked their way

down the rough path from the cave. "You were right all along," he said.

They made their way alone, keeping near the lake shore, following the path that had led them there. They stopped at the same place they had stopped the night before. It was not far from the cliff caverns, but it was far enough. There was a small, deceptive sense of freedom in being just this far from the cave of the Grooks.

The following morning they stopped at a Grook village and were fed. They moved on. It took two days and another night to make their way back to the ship. There was no need to hurry. There were no goals left to them.

At the clearing they saw the marks where the patrol ship had stood only a few hours before. Unconsciously, Morten stooped to feel the ground that had borne the weight of the ship. Arlee picked up a scrap of paper one of the patrolmen had dropped. Charred debris in a twenty-meter circle showed the effects of the ship's arrival and departure.

They moved silently away as if leaving a shrine and came to their own ship. The patrolmen had not bothered to close the hatch. It swung open as it had the night the Grooks had forced them out. They climbed the companionway to the cabin deck. Inside their room the bed and clothes remained in the disarray that had marked their hasty departure.

"I'll clear this up." Arlee moved absently.

Morten nodded. He moved toward the companionway and climbed to the pilot's compartment. Somehow, he had hoped the patrolmen might leave some message for them. A promise, perhaps, to return and check once again at some future date. But there was none. Their duty had been completed by the landing and the six-hour wait.

Morten entered the pilot's compartment. It had come to be a kind of sanctuary for him, even though its instruments lay dead and useless in their panels. He still half hoped a message might have been left, say, on the navigation table. That would be a likely place. But there was nothing still, no sign the place had been visited since he was last there.

He started to take a step toward the observation port. He wanted to see again the spot from which the patrol ship had taken off. He stopped in midstride. He stared at the equipment racks in a moment of disbelief. Then he ran to the companionway and called to his wife. "Arlee—come up, quickly!"

"I'm busy now. What is it?"

"Come up here!"

In a moment her head appeared above the floor level in answer to his fierce demand. "What do you want?"

"Arlee—come here." He took her hand and helped her up and led her aside so she could see the equipment racks. "Look at that!"

"What? I don't see—" Then she gasped. "The beacon—it's all right. It's not destroyed, after all! But we heard them—"

"Free must have done one last thing for us. Werk didn't know one piece of equipment from another. Free told him that was it, and so Werk smashed the navigator panels, thinking it was the beacon. Free gave us a chance once more."

"Then you can call the patrol back—if they will come."

"They'll come. They have to." Morten stepped to the beacon and switched it on. Apparently the patrolmen had found it running and had turned it off, for it would have been still running the night the Grooks had driven them out. He pressed the manual control and cut out the tape.

"Cephon II. Cephon II. Morten Bradwell calling Cephon II—"

He listened and waited. The hiss of space was the only signal coming through. Maybe they were busy on some other channel. But the emergency channels were supposed to be open always.

As the minutes passed, Arlee crumpled before the denied hope again. "I'll get some food for us," she said finally.

Morten continued calling. Perhaps the patrolmen had concluded it was only some hoax and were refusing to answer. But they couldn't do that, either. They were obligated to answer. Arlee brought food, and they ate together on the navigation table while Morten kept up the routine of calling and listening.

"I'll put the automatic tape back on and try again in the morning," he said finally.

And then, as if that were the cue that had been awaited, the voice came through from space. "Cephon II calling. Captain Reynolds speaking. We regret the delay in answering. Our main and backup transmitters were both out temporarily. We hear you, Bradwell. Come in."

Morten switched to transmission and told of their situation. "We saw you from our captivity across the lake. We'll barricade ourselves in the ship until you return. Take precautions when you land. Prepare for hostilities. We are armed with boron guns and sufficient ammunition. I hope we don't have to fire on the Grooks, but they are determined we shall not leave."

"We understand," said the patrol Captain. "We'll take precautions against hostilities. This time, we'll pick you up!"

Morten switched back to automatic transmission to guide the patrol, and slumped in his chair. He smiled wanly to Arlee. "We're going home, now. We really are."

"And Free—what of Free?"

"A few hours ago I would have said I didn't care. Now it is different. He deceived Werk in order to give us a chance to contact the patrol again. He cares enough for us to do that. We can't abandon him. He's going back with us!"

XIV

They prepared to retire, but as the night came on with tropical density they became aware of an intense glow in the night sky. It centered above the beach down by the Grook villages where Morten had turned off when he was first captured.

"Something big is going on," said Arlee. "I wonder if Free is there."

"Most likely." Morten procured the binoculars and went back to the upper level of the ship. He opened the work hatch and stood on the parapet. Arlee came up beside him. "Can you tell what's going on?"

"Take a look," he said.

Arlee took the glasses and steadied herself against the hull of the ship. In the glow of intense firelight she could see the activities on the beach quite clearly. A kind of procession was moving slowly about the immense fire. Figures outside the procession were dancing with wild gestures. The sound of their chanting and singing came faintly through the night.

"They're carrying something," she said. "They're

carrying something around the fire, a kind of platform. Somebody is sitting on the platform on something like a throne."

Morten waited for her to go on.

"It's Free!" she said. "They're carrying Free around the fire like a king—or a sacrifice—"

Morten nodded. "He's the Star Prince at last. This is what he stayed for. He knew it was coming."

"Then—why not leave him? Why even consider taking him back with us? Why, he's got a place of security and renown with these natives. Nothing you could ever offer him in civilization would match that."

Morten leaned on the parapet railing and watched the distant firelight. "Even you don't really believe that, Arlee," he said. "This is just another King of Eolim. It has no more meaning than the mockery he experienced in school. To be a king among savages is no more than being a fool among superiors."

"It is, Morten! You've become so blinded by your ambition to raise him to levels he can never attain that you can't see the worth of what he can be and do."

"If that were true why do you think I gave up my whole life and career to bring him out to Randor, where he would be with his kind."

"He has found his kind," said Arlee. "The Grooks are his kind, and you refuse to admit it. Among them he has found his own level and a place of achievement. He's the Star Prince—through some wonderful coincidence of their legends and his own delusions. No matter how you look at it, it's something wonderful for him. If you really love him you'll let him remain, without trying to force some imagined civilized improvements on him. He has found what he's always dreamed of. The Star Prince has come home."

"You make it sound as if you are delighted for him and his success—after the bitterness you've held for him all his life."

"Nothing has changed for me. It is just so apparent that you are blindly forcing him in a direction you want. Perhaps I have been equally as blind in seeing no worth in him. Perhaps he deserves far better than either of us."

Morten felt astonishment at the sense of compassion in Arlee's words, yet he supposed it was inspired only by the hope that Free would be left among the Grooks, and she would be rid of him forever.

"Let's go down," he said, turning away. "Perhaps Free will come to the ship tomorrow and tell us all about it."

They retired at last, exhausted from their experience with the Grooks and weary of trying to reach a decision about Free. The following day they took up their preparations for leaving, where they had left off before the invasion of the Grooks. They packed what was essential and left what they had learned they could do without.

The next day, in the late afternoon, Free appeared. He was alone, and he was wearing a red cape decorated with bird feathers, and a headdress that was like a helmet of gold and red feathers. Morten and Arlee were outside in the clearing when he appeared. He was exuberant, and his face shone with a kind of joy that Morten had never seen in him before.

"I am the Star Prince," said Free. "The Grooks knew it, too. That is why they wouldn't let you take me away. Last night they held a big ceremony and crowned me their Star Prince."

"We saw it," said Morten. "It reminded us of when you were made King of Eolim."

"Yes," said Free. "It was like that, only so much better. This was real. Now I'm really the Star Prince, and these are my people. I will keep the evil of the *baru* from them. And now you can go back, and maybe some day you will come and see me again. I saved the beacon for you when Werk wanted to destroy it. You saw that, didn't you?"

"We discovered it, and we are grateful," said Morten.

"Is the patrol ship on the way back?"

"They'll be here again in a couple of days."

"They won't bother the Grooks, like Werk feared, will they?"

"No. No one will bother the Grooks. I promise you that."

"I want to stay here tonight and then I'll take my things that I want to keep in the morning."

"Sure, Free. That's fine. Come and eat with us now. We have dinner just about ready."

Free removed his treasured cape and headdress and took them to his cabin in the ship. Arlee turned to Morten. "What are you going to do? He's taking it for granted that he's staying."

"I'm going to change his mind about that," said Morten.

It seemed pleasant that evening in the clearing. Almost like an old-fashioned picnic, Morten thought.

He had read about times when people went out to the natural countryside like this and ate their meals in a kind of celebration or holiday. In a way this was a holiday celebration, too. The celebration of the Star Prince. The celebration of their return to civilization.

It grew dark and they built up a fire to keep back the night. The sounds of night beasts rose in the forest. The smooth waters of the lake were broken occasionally by some creature from the depths. Morten thought of the carcass of the *baru*, which had long since disintegrated out there. He wondered how many more of the beasts there might be in the depths of the water.

Insects were attracted by the light of the fire, and they buzzed into it with flaming sparks. Morten glanced at his watch. "Time to turn in, I guess. Let the fire die down and we'll call it a day."

They retreated to the ship, leaving dim coals behind them.

"Don't stumble over the luggage," said Morten. "We've put it all near the hatch so it will be ready to grab when the ship comes."

"You've got one of mine there," said Free.

"Well, yes, so we have. Just leave it, and you can get it in the morning."

They were awakened at dawn by Free's angry and anguished cry. He burst into their cabin. "You've put locks on the hatches!" he cried. "You think I'm leaving with you!"

"I'm afraid you're right," said Morten gently. "I've thought it over very carefully, and it's still not right that you should spend your life among these savages. You have more worth than that."

"I'm their Star Prince now! You can't take the Star Prince away from them!"

"I don't know about any Star Prince, Free. All I know is I'm taking my son back to civilization with me."

"I saved the beacon so you could get away—and now you do this to me."

"There would have been no capture by the Grooks if you hadn't let them know the patrol was coming. But there's no use arguing what either of us have done. I gave up my life and my career to see you located in a place where you could be happy and have the benefits of civilization. In the years to come, you will thank me, no matter how bitter you may be now."

"When are they coming?"

"Day after tomorrow evening they should be here."

"You lied to me, Dad! You lied to me!" Free turned with a cry of anguish and ran from the room.

Arlee said. "You've lost him. You'll never get him back."

"You may be right. But it will be best for him in the long run."

All day Free avoided Morten in the self-imposed prison of the ship. Toward evening, when Morten was busy with his daily contact with the patrol ship, Free sought out Arlee, who was in the lounge.

He approached from the lower level companionway and stood behind her a long time as she reclined on the lounge, reading. She became aware of his presence and turned with annoyance. "Why are you standing there? What do you want, Free?"

He hesitated, almost stammering. "I want to talk to you, Mom."

172

"Come ahead. Sit over here on this chair. What do you want to talk to me about?" She spoke rapidly, as if she had to put a barrier of words between them to ease their discomfort.

Free sat uneasily on the edge of the chair. "You don't want me to go back with you, do you? You want me to stay here, don't you?"

"I think you would be much happier here. I realize you are fond of the Grooks and they admire you. You were never this happy in any circumstances on Earth, were you?"

"No. I want to stay. This is where I belong. Open the door and let me go out. Give me what we both want!"

His mother shook her head. "Your father has sealed them. I can't open them. Only he can do that."

"You could be rid of me forever. Wouldn't it be worth opening the ship so you would never have to bother with me again?"

"Free—! I told you—"

He leaned forward in a sudden burst of pent-up rage. "Don't act so surprised. Don't you think I've always known how you felt about me since I was a little boy? You wanted me dead, didn't you? You wanted them to kill me as soon as I was born so you wouldn't have to bother with me.

"I *know* what happens to Retards like me. I may be too stupid to learn in school, but I'm not too dumb to have learned what they do to Retards. And I know it was Dad who wanted to keep me, and you wanted to do away with me."

Arlee shrank before the rage that flowed out of the boy. She had never been confronted with his awareness of his condition. She had never heard him speak except in the mildest of tones.

"You have never thought of me as a human being, have you?" he demanded. "Have you—? Tell me—?"

"Free, I—"

"Do you think I'm any different from you? I'm not. I'm human, too. I get happy, and I get sad. And I want friends and people who like me. The Grooks like me. That's more than anybody on Earth ever did. That's more than you ever did. Dad is the only one who ever cared anything about me—but he doesn't understand how much I need to stay here."

There were tears in his eyes. He was trying to hold them back, but could not. It frightened her a little. She couldn't remember if she had seen him cry before or not. He must have done so when he was a baby, but she couldn't recall it.

He was straining to keep from crying now, and his rage helped. But the crying was like tearing away a shroud that had concealed him. Suddenly she saw *him*. She put out a hand awkwardly. "Free—"

He started up and fled from the room. But at the doorway he stopped and cried out, "You wanted me dead. You killed me!"

He disappeared into the lower parts of the ship. Arlee remained where she sat, shaken by his outburst. She couldn't rid her mind of the image of his tearful face, or the ringing of his words, "I'm human, too."

It was a revelation of something she had never experienced before: Free—a human being. She recognized with a kind of little horror that she had never thought of him as human in the same way she and Morten and their genetically engineered friends

174

were human. He had always been something only a little above animal.

Were all Retards like this? she wondered. Did they all cry? Did they get angry? Did they want love?

Was it possible a mistake had been made in the treatment of the Retards? It seemed inconceivable. Retards were the debris of creation. Their slow, dull-witted natures could not be allowed to contaminate the civilization of normals. Yet—they cried, and they loved.

Was that the criteria for human classification as much or more than brilliance of mind and swiftness of intellect?

There were not may Retards any more. No more than a few hundred a year. All but a handful went to the euthanasia chambers. Did it represent that many cold-blooded murders?

For Free, she thought with a sudden, choking pain inside her, it would have been murder.

Morten returned from the pilot's compartment, his steps clattering on the metal stairs. "The patrol is on schedule. It looks as if nothing can possibly interfere with our leaving this time."

Arlee continued staring at the wall without answering.

"What's the matter?" asked Morten. "Are you all right?"

"You're not really going to force Free to go with us, are you?"

"Of course I am. We've been over this enough times before."

"You have said you want to do whatever will make him happy and well. I think taking him away from here is the cruelest possible thing you could do to him."

Morten sat on the lounge across from his wife. "Why do you say that? You haven't cared much up to now whether he was happy or miserable. Why are you concerned now? Is it because you can't stand him with us any longer at all?"

"I know I deserve that," said Arlee, "but I've changed just a bit since we last talked about Free."

"How? What changed you?"

"I saw him cry."

He wondered if she were mocking him. He started to speak and then hesitated. He became aware that her own eyes were strangely close to tears. Surely it couldn't be concerning Free—

"What was he crying about?"

"Himself—his loneliness, his need of love, his total rejection as a human being. He cried because he knew I wanted him dead."

Morten's anger flared. "You told him that?"

"No. I didn't tell him. I didn't have to. He knows all about what happens to Retards. Somehow he found out."

"It wouldn't be hard, I suppose." Morten subsided in grimness. "What a hell he must live in—and others like him who know what they are."

"Morten—when I saw him cry it was as if I were seeing him for the first time. I saw a human being. I realized that Free is a human being. I've never thought of a Retard that way before. I never have!"

"And so you want to leave him here."

"Yes—because he's happy here. He loves these people and they love him.

"It might make him equally happy if his mother told him she loved him."

Arlee looked down at her hands, her eyes wet, "I might be able to do that—in time. I'm not ready yet."

"If you were, his leaving the Grooks might be a lot easier."

"But why must he leave?"

"We've gone over it endless times," said Morten irritably. "There's no use rehearsing it again. I refuse to abandon him to savagery. He's got to have some degree of civilization to develop such potential as he has."

"Civilization wants him dead."

"You are deliberately misunderstanding me. And I don't understand what's happened to you, Arlee. All his life you've wanted him destroyed. You wanted to leave him here to get him out of your way. Now you insist you want to leave him for his own good, because he can find happiness here."

"I don't fully understand myself, Morten." Arlee got up and moved to the port hole to glance at the dying sun. "Please think of what I've asked. Let's not talk about it any more, now."

XV

Arlee prepared a meal. Free reappeared from the lower levels of the ship. Morten tried to make conversation, but the meal passed mostly in stony silence.

As darkness grew outside and blacked out the port holes, a flicker of light appeared. Morten strode to the porthole of the lounge and looked out. Torches appeared in the clearing, and a surge of dark bodies could be seen. Morten strained his eyes and shaded them. Then he began to distinguish more and more of the moving shapes. Grooks. An incredible number of them. Hundreds. Perhaps thousands.

"Free!" he demanded. "What are the Grooks doing out there? Did you call them?"

The boy shook his head sullenly. "I didn't call them. I told them I was going to be taken away, and they came by themselves."

"Why did you have to tell them anything? What are they going to do? Are they going to attack us?"

"No. You don't need to be afraid of them. You'll

soon see what they are going to do. It should be a good show for you."

Morten's rage surged within him. He wasn't even behaving rationally, he thought. The imminence of the patrol ship's landing was unnerving him. He had built such hopes the last time. Now, the ship was approaching once more, and the clearing was filled with Grooks. Did they intend to oppose the landing simply by filling up the space? If that was it, he'd instruct the patrol to land on top of them. With the boron guns he could clear a way between the ships. But there seemed to be something more to their presence than mere silent opposition. Free knew what it was.

Fires were lit to augment the torches, and now he could see there was truly an enormous, milling crowd of the natives, even more than he had at first supposed.

Arlee shuddered. "They frighten me. Do you have any idea why they are here?"

"No. Free does, but he won't tell us. He's unmanageable since living with them. He behaves as savagely as they do. I think that's proof enough of what he would become if he stayed."

Arlee made no answer. She didn't want to resume that argument again. She watched the Grooks.

Morten was sure the Grooks had come to rescue Free. How they intended to do it he had no idea, and it angered him beyond reason because he was sure Free did know.

They appeared to be starting some organized task. Groups of them dispersed and returned quickly with lengths of logs and dead trees. There were many of

180

these in large piles of debris taken from the clearing. Now the Grooks brought back vast quantities and began building a pile between the ship and the lake shore.

It was like two walls of brush and timber forming a V, with the open end toward the ship and the point towards the lake. The walls did not come entirely to a closed point; only a narrow space was left at the tip of the V.

Free had returned now and, without speaking, watched from one of the ports. Morten refused to ask him again what the Grooks intended. Arlee stood beside Morten, her hand trembling on the edge of the port. "Isn't there some way we can get the patrol here faster—before those savages finish whatever they're doing?"

"Unless the Grooks endanger us I don't want to bother the patrol any more. They'll be making the best possible speed and they're not too happy with us anyway, even though it's not our fault they have had to come twice to pick us up."

Arlee turned to Free. "Won't you tell us what they're going to do?"

"It's not going to hurt us." Free's face was tight. His mouth was set in grimness they had not seen before. "You'll see in a little while."

It had taken a long time to build the V-shaped pile of debris. It was past midnight when the structure was done. He recognized among the workers some of those who had been in his class. And he recognized Werk, who seemed to be among the most energetic of the Grooks.

Morten could tell that Free was watching his

friend also; his face became more tense and drawn as Werk appeared in view.

When the structure was finally complete, the Grooks tossed buckets of liquid over the piles. It appeared oily, and Morten thought it must be oil.

The natives grouped themselves about the open end, ranging about the ship and on all sides except the back, away from the pile. They were all in sight of the open V of the brush and timber structure. A double line of torch bearers faced one another, a half dozen meters apart in front of the wide end of the V.

The chanting began then, slowly, almost inaudibly. No one moved. Immobile, the torch bearers faced one another.

There was no leader for the song that alternately chanted and wailed, but the voices were in complete unison as if they had rehearsed a lifetime for this moment. The sound raged toward a crescendo of ululation and vanished abruptly. Nothing followed. It seemed as if a blank in time had occurred.

Then the torch bearers moved. They crept toward the V, as if reluctant to approach it. The light of their torches flickered over the taut faces of the assembled Grooks. As the men came to the line that marked the entrance to the V, however, a cry erupted from the Grook throats in a shrill disharmony. The torch bearers leaped in a frenzy of motion and wildly plunged their torches into the piles of oiled wood and brush.

The debris burst into yellow, smoky flame that raced through the pile. The torch bearers tried to race ahead of it, plunging their flames from point to point until the whole structure was afire. Yellow light brightened the clearing in flickering, plunging bursts. The men raced toward the narrow end, where already the flames had closed the gap. They surged through the flames, flinging their torches high into the walls of fire as they escaped. They ran on the outside of the pile and returned to their places.

The flames roared against the sky. Crews of Grook fire keepers were on either side, replacing the fuel as it began to burn down.

There was no movement from the watching Grooks. They began to sing again, a low, wailing lament as if doom had overtaken them. There was a sense of pleading, Morten thought, and he wondered if it was directed at him. Free continued to watch, his set expression unchanging. Arlee remained staring, waiting for something to happen; she didn't know what.

Suddenly, one of the Grooks in the front of the assembly leaped up. He ran to the opening of the V, then halted, looking at the walls of fire on either side. He turned and bowed ceremoniously to the group, then looked up to the ship as if he knew the Earthlings were watching. He extended an arm in salute.

Free's mouth tightened. The Grook turned about slowly and began walking with measured steps toward the point of the V. Arlee cried out, "He's walking into the fire!"

Morten's face was stretched tight across his cheekbones. This is what he had known would happen; he had suspected from the beginning.

The Grook did not falter as his steps took him forward and the flames reached for him from either side. They touched him. He seemed enveloped in a halo of surging light. Steadily, he moved on until the light enclosed him and only a shadow could be seen through the yellow tongues of fire. The shadow faltered, twisted as if in some melancholy dance, and then dropped from sight.

The Grooks voices rose in wild lament.

Almost instantly, another figure separated itself from the group and approached the V.

Arlee turned as if to hide the vision from her sight. "They can't go on like that! Why do they do it? What is it all for?"

Free faced them. "You wanted to know what they intended to do! Now you know. It's a little like the euthanasia chamber, isn't it? The Grooks are Retards —they should be destroyed. Isn't that what your great genetically engineered culture says? Why don't you let me go now so that I can join them and walk into the fire with my friends?"

"Free!" Morten whirled upon him. "You're talking with total unreason."

"Do you expect any more from a Retard?"

They heard the awful lament from the Grook voices once again and knew that another shadow had vanished in the flames.

Abruptly, Free seemed to shrink. The harsh belligerency left his face and was replaced by the agonized appeal of recent days. "Don't you understand, Dad? They're doing it for me. They're doing it to try to save their Star Prince."

"I understand well enough," said Morten. "It's a savage gesture, the kind of thing to expect from the

184

mentality represented out there. It's a gesture totally unrelated to the goal they're trying to achieve."

Arlee was staring out at the flaming V once again. The Grook voices lamented and wailed. "It is very much different?" she said quietly to Morten. "Is it really different from our euthanasia chambers? Is our mentality so much greater than theirs?"

"Arlee! What kind of nonsense is that. Our euthanasia program has a rational purpose, even if I don't agree with it entirely. It's a rational approach to a problem. Do you see any rationality out there?" He flung an arm in the direction of the Grooks.

"I don't know, Morten. I just don't know. But let Free go to his people. He'll never find happiness with us. And those natives will continue walking into the flames until they're all gone."

"Let them!"

Free gripped his arms and stared into his face with pleading in his eyes. "You don't know what it's like, Dad. Try to understand Just try to understand what it's like to be King of Eolim!"

"What do you mean? I thought you liked that?"

"Dad—I'm stupid, but I'm not a fool. Don't you think I know what King of Eolim means? Don't you think I know I was being picked as the stupidest person in school. I knew it—and I couldn't bear it. The only way I could bear it was to make people think I believed it to be an honor. It cut off their pity and they couldn't act like there was anything to be sorry for. Not to my face, anyway. They congratulated me. That's the way it was the night of the party at home. Everybody told me it was great. But they knew what

185

it meant. And so did you. And so did I. You don't know what it's like to be King of Eolim!"

"Free—"

"Dad, you're so far above me there is no way we can live in the same world. In yours I'll always be King of Eolim. Here, among the Grooks, I'm the Star Prince. You want me to be a normal human being in your world. I can't. Only among the Grooks am I normal. Somehow I'm Grook, not human. Can't you understand, Dad?"

Morten turned away without answering. He watched again a shadowy Grook body disappearing into the flaming light. His hopes for Free seemed to be vanishing in those flames. He had been ready to sacrifice his career and all the rest of his years to give Free a normal, human life, but it meant nothing to the boy.

But Morten remembered the night of Free's irrational effort to appear in acceptable guise by donning his King of Eolim crown and appearing among the guests at the soirée. Morten had thought it a mere misguided, childish act. Now he understood something of the agony that must have led Free to do it.

Suddenly Free gave a loud cry and pointed to the natives below.

"Werk! Werk is going into the fire!"

Morten brought his attention back. Free's young Grook friend was getting to his feet and striding slowly toward the flaming V.

"Dad! Werk—he's offering his life to get me back —their Star Prince—in the only way he knows how. He's doing it for me. Would you ever do as much to help me—?"

Arlee touched Morten's arm. "You've got to stop them—"

Morten suddenly reached out and embraced Free fiercely. "Yes. I'll do as much. I'll do more than any of them. A thousand times more. Remember that, Free."

He raced down the companion way. At the lowest level he released the lock and flung the hatch open. Behind him, Free stared as if he didn't comprehend. Arlee was beside him. Then Free embraced Morten fiercely. "I love you, Dad."

He put his arms about Arlee and kissed her. "I love you, Mom."

She stiffened, then her arms clutched him hungrily and held him. She pressed her face against his. "I love you, Free. I love you—my son."

"Mom—Mom—" He rocked from side to side, holding her tightly in his arms. Then he broke away and stood in the hatchway. "Werk—I've got to get to him!"

He looked a moment, fixing their images in his mind. "Remember me. I'll think of you forever."

He ran from the ship into the crowd of Grooks outside. Morten closed the hatch and locked it tight once more. Arlee clutched his arm and held close to him. "Thank you, Morten. Thank you with all my heart."

"Let's see what happens. They've got to stop Werk."

They returned to the upper level ports. A cry such as they had never heard from the Grooks was rising now from the great mass of natives below. A cry of joy. Of release. Of exultation.

It started at the base of the ship, among the nucleus who saw Free come out. It spread faster than the fire through the remainder of the crowd.

It reached Werk, who stood in the midst of the searing fires. He turned as the sound reached his ears. Then through the mass he saw a figure. Free was racing forward as the crowd parted. He ran with open arms into the funnel of the V. Werk ran to meet him. They embraced like brothers near the heat of the flames while the Grooks roared in exultation.

Morten turned away from the port and held Arlee close to him. "He's gone. Whether it was the right thing or the wrong, we'll never know."

"Yes, we will," said Arlee. "We know it now. We could never give him what those people out there are giving him. He was right. He is one of them, not one of us."

"He forgot his cape," said Morten. "His cape and headdress. We'll have to take them with us—to remember the Star Prince."

When the patrol ship landed the next day there was no sign of the Grooks in the clearing. But the great pyre was still smoldering. Captain Reynolds looked at the charred remains as Morten and Arlee came across the clearing to meet the patrolmen.

"You must have had a mighty big barbecue to celebrate your leaving. That's enough fire to burn down half the planet."

"It was a kind of celebration," said Morten. "We decided to leave our son here. He was adopted by the local citizens and is going to remain."

The patrolman looked at him quizzically. "You're sure that's all right? We have to report on all missing citizens, and there'll be a lot of paper work to process."

"It's all right," said Morten. "He was a Retard, you see. No one will miss him."

From space, the planet resembled Earth just a little. It was green and blue and flecked with white clouds. The shapes of continents were entirely different, of course.

"I don't understand his illusion," said Morten as the planet dwindled. "How could he have believed he had seen life elsewhere as the Star Prince—and be convinced this primitive planet was it?"

"Even more—" said Arlee. "How did it come to coincide with the traditions of the Grooks that their Star Prince was coming some day to rule and protect them?"

"I wonder if there are qualities and abilities our genetic processes introduce at random that we never recognize. Perhaps there was something here, after all, that let Free reach out and know things that ordinary human senses never discern."

"Who knows but that some tenuous link between the stars exists beyond our understanding?" said Arlee. "Maybe some link stretched between here and Earth linking Free and this people together. Perhaps this link was somehow responsible for our crashing in this particular place—so that the Grooks might gain their Star Prince."

Morten glanced at his wife to see if she were mocking him. Her face was sober as she looked out upon the stars.

"You surely don't believe any such ridiculous thing," said Morten.

"I wonder," said Arlee. "Yes, I think I do be-lieve it."

Morten knew, then, that his wife was changing, perhaps against her will but changing nevertheless. He felt momentary regret that this had not happened while Free was still with them.

Free. . . .

My son, my son, he thought. May God be with you . . . with us all.

Secretly he wept. For while he tried to pretend that the fact of his son's new, vibrant happiness would ease his own sorrow, he also knew what the truth was, and that truth hurt more than anything else had in many, many years.

He looked at Arlee, hard-hearted, self-centered at first but now there was a curious sensitivity in her expression, her own eyes moist around the edges.

"We'll try," she said, anticipating him. "God knows we'll try."

He nodded and embraced his wife.

Free was sitting with his head bowed when Werk approached him.

"Is there anything wrong, my friend?" the Grook asked, since Free's thoughts were strangely turbulent, hard to fathom.

The human looked up—and there were tears in his eyes.

Nothing more had to be said.

DON'T MISS ANY OF THESE EXCITING
LASER BOOKS

READ ABOUT MORE EXCITING TITLES ON THE NEXT PAGE!

No. 9 Invasion by Aaron Wolfe

> A spine-tingling tale of one family's struggles against a band of marauding alien creatures with murder on their minds.

No. 10 Falling Toward Forever by Gordon Eklund

> A mercenary soldier-of-fortune battles his unknown manipulator as he is flung from one time period to another.

No. 11 Unto The Last Generation by Juanita Coulson

> A little girl brings hope to a team of scientists trying to heal mankind's total sterility.

No. 12 The King of Eolim by Raymond F. Jones

> A deeply sensitive story about a family whose retarded son is not tolerated by society. A masterful adventure!

USE THIS HANDY FORM TO ORDER YOUR BOOKS